McPHEE GRIBBLE/PENGUIN

COLOURING IN
A Book of Ideologically Unsound Love Stories

Jean Bedford was born in England in 1946 and, after coming to Australia, grew up in rural Victoria. She has worked as a journalist, book reviewer, teacher and most recently as literary consultant to the Australian Film Commission. Her first collection of short stories *Country Girl Again* appeared in 1979, followed by the novels *Sister Kate* in 1982 and *Love Child* in 1986. Jean Bedford lives in Sydney and has three daughters.

Rosemary Creswell was born in Sydney in 1941. She has worked in advertising, radio, as a teaching fellow in the English Department at the University of Sydney and currently works as a literary agent. She has published book reviews and literary criticism in a range of newspapers and magazines. This is her first published work of fiction.

Colouring In

A Book of
Ideologically Unsound
Love Stories

JEAN BEDFORD
and
ROSEMARY CRESWELL

McPHEE GRIBBLE/PENGUIN BOOKS

McPhee Gribble Publishers Pty Ltd
66 Cecil Street
Fitzroy, Victoria, 3065, Australia

Penguin Books Australia Ltd,
487 Maroondah Highway, P.O. Box 257
Ringwood, Victoria, 3134, Australia
Penguin Books Ltd,
Harmondsworth, Middlesex, England
Penguin Books,
40 West 23rd Street, New York, N.Y. 10010, U.S.A.
Penguin Books Canada Ltd,
2801 John Street, Markham, Ontario, Canada L3R IB4
Penguin Books (N.Z.) Ltd,
182–190 Wairau Road, Auckland 10, New Zealand

First published by McPhee Gribble Publishers
in association with Penguin Books Australia, 1986
Copyright © Jean Bedford and Rosemary Creswell, 1986

Typeset in Bembo by Bookset, Melbourne
Made and printed in Australia by
The Dominion Press–Hedges & Bell

National Library of Australia
Cataloguing-in-Publication data
Bedford, Jean, 1946-
Colouring In: A Book of Ideologically Unsound
Love Stories
ISBN 0 14 009675 2
1. Short stories, Australian. I.
Creswell, Rosemary 1941- II. Title.
A823'.0108

Contents

Campaign

Jean Bedford

I'd been on a binge with Iris for most of the week. Now I woke up in the hot morning still drunk. Somehow I'd pulled up the quilt in the night and I was sweating.

My daughter Sarah looked in at me with one of her fifteen-year old looks. She was home studying but I noticed *Dune* under her arm and gave her one of my forty-year old looks. It hurt when I laughed.

'I thought you were going out to lunch?'

'I am.' I looked at the clock; I was already half an hour late.

'Get me two Panadol. Quick.'

I showered and dressed. I don't usually wear too much makeup but now I needed heaps. Too old to drink all night, I decided. Time to dry out. I rang the restaurant and left a message for Harry, then I rang a cab. The walk up the road to hail one was too daunting.

Harry was going to introduce me to a Yugoslav attaché, so I could get invited to Belgrade. My friend Iris said he was my type. Iris was in love; she thought I should be, too. I thought I didn't want to fall in love again, but if I did, I said to Iris and Harry in the wine bar one night, this time I wanted it to my exact specifications.

'A French diplomat,' I'd said. 'Preferably half Jewish. Married once, perhaps been gay. Rich, sophisticated, a

1

lot older. He'll take me to Paris for holidays and buy heaps of champagne.'

'I can do you a Yugoslav,' Harry said. 'At least he might get you invited to the Belgrade festival.'

'That'll do. Love's fucked, anyway.' We all laughed – our young friend Moira was going through a phase of telling us that everything was fucked just then.

Harry was at his usual table, with people I didn't know. I was the only woman. I noticed Tom and sat beside him. I don't like to be at Harry's table with just strangers, they always intimidate me, talking politics and corruption with Harry.

'He didn't come,' Harry said. 'Perhaps I should have rung him back. *I* don't understand Yugoslav protocol.'

I'd forgotten the Yugoslav, so I laughed and went on talking to Tom, drinking the first glass of wine quickly to stop the shakes. It was one of Harry's lunches; he's famous for them. Eclectic and jovial, socially, politically, intellectually omniverous, Harry collects very good lunches.

There was a retired American colonel canvassing for the Australian Democrats; there was his shadow from *Newsweek*; there were a couple of men who were probably lawyers or politicians, another whom I knew to be a judge. And Tom, an old friend. I was pleased to see him and catch up on gossip. There was also a youngish man beside Tom but he didn't talk much and I only got glimpses of him when Tom leaned forward to pour another drink. Most of the talk was of the election, now a month off.

Tom paid for my lunch and cashed a cheque for me and we thought we might all go somewhere and have a palate-cleansing ale, Harry's expression that he said he'd got from Ernest. The youngish man invited us back to campaign headquarters – he was working for a Victorian politician. I remembered I'd met him before, he'd said he liked my book. He looked tired. His name was Tony something, I thought.

So we had our beers there while Tom called clients in Perth and Melbourne and Harry called other people. I was bored with the election, I wondered why I was there, but it was pleasant drinking cold beer a long way above the hot city, with the storms starting again. I thought idly that if this had been America we'd have all been rich.

Tom left and Harry and I decided to share a taxi back to our suburb. He got up to go and I groaned at the thought of more travel.

'Don't go,' Tony said to me. 'Have another beer.'

Harry waited, and I thought, Why not?

'You coming, Sal?'

'No, I'll stay.'

On Monday morning I went into Iris's office. She was on the phone as usual. It was nearly lunchtime so I waited while she harrassed publishers, dealt patiently with clients.

'Well,' she said in the wine bar. 'Are you going to Belgrade?'

'Nah,' I said. 'Belgrade's fucked. But . . .' I poured the wine, 'I think I'm falling in love.'

Iris laughed. I always said that at first and then the next day, or the next week, I'd deny I ever said it.

'Who with? Do I know him?' Iris knows it's always a him.

I told her and we settled down to girl talk. I wondered if I usually said 'This is different. I feel it.' I didn't think so, I didn't think I'd had this for years. I was starting to obsess. I was even getting interested in the election.

'Tactics,' I said. 'I've never been good at them, but I need some now.' I didn't really think I did. I felt confident.

3

'I even took him down to the beach house,' I said. 'That'll show him. Kids and dogs and ex-husbands everywhere, and a party where all my com mates put shit on him. That'll show what he's made of.'

I thought I was beginning to know what he was made of. I'd found his verbal reticence off-putting at first, wondered if I was bored, if it had been a mistake to invite him to the beach. I thought he was very tense and uncertain, I wondered if I intimidated him. But I'd seen him fence with my coastal friends, watched his smile when people got illogical or brought out cant. I'd liked the way we stood squeezed together all night, feeling each other up like teenagers. I'd laughed at my friend Mary's sardonic disapproval. Mary doesn't believe in being in love, especially, she said, with a State apparatchik. I'd liked the way, when we were lying on the beach, he had stroked the hair on my neck.

I said something to Iris about feeling vulnerable again.

'I don't know if I remember how you do it,' I said.

'No. You've got guarded.' She laughed, 'Don't tell him I told you but Alec said once that you hardly ever kissed him.'

'No.' I was struck by that. 'He's right. I hardly ever did. It's like whores, isn't it? Alright to fuck and suck and everything else, but kissing's too intimate.'

'It lets them into your head,' Iris said.

'I don't think I've kissed anyone properly since Robert,' I said. 'Oh well. Tactics are fucked, too. He knows where to find me.'

Well, he found me, we found each other, I thought. I started to learn to kiss again, and stare at someone's eyes. He brought champagne and presents, I bought him red roses. My kids told him he looked spunky in his suit. Leo, who shared my house, told him it was sickening to see me so happy. We had our jokes, we watched videos, we drank, fucked, talked. I did no work, I waited the days through to see him. I didn't believe it but I wanted it to be true. I didn't think of the future, the future's fucked, I said to Iris. We scandalised the waiters at Kinselas. 'Wanton behaviour,' said the nice fair one, with pursed lips. He'd often poured us out at three a.m. after rowdy drunken dinners, but no-one approved of love.

Then, near election day, at dinner, he said, 'I'm worried about your expectations.'

'I've got none. Really.' Just – let this go on.

'I can't handle it. It's my fault. I didn't mean to let it happen. It's dangerous and I can't go on with it.'

I knew about his girlfriend, of course, but she was in another city. I only wanted what we had, I wasn't interested in the rest.

'But to stop. So suddenly.'

'It happened suddenly.'

'Straight in, straight out?' I watched his impatience at my bitchiness.

'We can be mates still.'

'Can we?' I stared at him. 'Is this how you make *all* your friends?'

He stared back. 'No.' he said. 'No, it's not.'

I'd intended not to talk about it at all, to be gallant, give in gracefully. Now I had all sorts of pride, hurt, defensiveness struggling out of me. I'd had too much to drink, I was confused. I couldn't help trying to fight for myself. Even though I knew fighting for yourself is fucked, when the other has already left the field.

'I don't know,' I said, 'if I can be your friend.'

It gave me some satisfaction that this seemed to hurt him. He was tired, as usual. I really didn't want to hassle.

'Did you ever tell him you were in love with him?' Iris

5

said. 'Perhaps that would have helped.'

'No.' I said. 'It would have made it worse. I think. I tried to cover myself in the end. I can't *make* him want me if he doesn't. I bloody wish I could, but.'

'Well, you can cry on my shoulder,' she said. 'It might not really be over.' .

'No. It's over. And I don't feel like crying on shoulders.'

We're friends now, I suppose we always were. We sometimes send each other postcards with lighthearted messages. I cut out obscure newspaper paragraphs that I think will interest him and he sometimes rings just to say hello. When he is in this city we meet for drinks, buy each other lunches, sometimes dinner – but not often, because the night-time is dangerous and besides it is to spend with the one you love.

Every now and then we are both at one of Harry's lunches. I never think – this is where we met. We gossip, I ask about his work, he asks about mine. I try to amuse him, I show off and am illogical, animated. He doesn't seem to mind – he likes me. We're fond of each other. He is his reserved self and I like that. I like his eyes and the way the smile breaks in his dark tired face. I like his honesty and his clear mind. It's good to have a friend like him.

I wrote him a poem recently but I haven't sent it. It's meant to make him laugh. It goes: If you're ever free, To fall in love with me, Please can I be, The first to know?

I'm going to say on the postcard, if I send it, 'This is a line from a short story I once wrote.'

Saturday Breakfast

Rosemary Creswell

Sometimes, there are some things that are hard to explain to men.

Phillip had spent the night with Iris. It had been a difficult night. A Friday night. But eventually they thought they had sorted things out. They had gone to dinner at a new Mexican restaurant. Phillip had noticed it when he got off the bus at Parramatta Road, Annandale, on his way to Iris's place for dinner.

The relationship was fairly new, so although it was a hot night Phillip wore a tie. As soon as Iris saw him she knew she was *pleased* to see him and so she knew it was real and she wasn't inventing it. She was *pleased* to see him in a tie. She was *pleased* to remember that he was tall and that he was a bit stiff and formal and shy.

He arrived at Iris's house with a punnet of strawberries, two mangoes, a bag of peaches, a bunch of carnations and a bottle of Mateus rosé, which neither of them, as it turned out, liked but which was on special at the corner bottleshop where the saleswoman had winked at him because of the gifts he was carrying. (It turned out, too, that it didn't matter that they didn't like rosé because the next week Iris's friend, Jenny, who was partial to rosé because she took a lot of drugs to control manic depressive psychosis and said that any other alcohol was no

7

good for her because it made her go to sleep, except for a couple of glasses of Scotch before bed along with the lithium to help her sleep, drank it all.)

Things got off to a bad start when they were having a beer in the back garden and Iris's dog, which was uncontrollable by anyone except Phillip (Jenny, who hated her girlfriends' boyfriends, had said, 'That'd be about his level, pitching his mind against a dog's') knocked over the carnations which Iris had arranged in a vase on the carefully set and candlelit dining-room table. So it had seemed better to eat out than to try to repair the mess.

At the restaurant, Phillip had questioned her whereabouts the previous evening, and was unsatisfied with her answers, though they were the truth. They had only been together for a month but they were in love. Iris had a friend called Otto. He was an old friend. He lived at Gosford up on the central coast most of the time with his wife and children and he worked a few days a week in Sydney. He was a short story writer and a freelance journalist. Otto was a bit of a drunk sometimes. The night before, on Thursday, he had called in on Iris at her office for some drinks, which she always had in the fridge, and because he was looking for Sal with whom he was having a friendly casual affair on his Sydney days, and Sal was often in Iris's office having some drinks. But Sal was in love with a new man, Tony, and wasn't there, and so Iris and Otto had dinner together in the wine bar down the road and were joined by Iris's friend Peg.

Iris didn't tell Otto about Sal's new love affair. She just said that she thought Sal was out to dinner somewhere – which she was, but with her new lover who was a political press secretary up in Sydney from Melbourne for an election campaign.

Apart from the more recent months, during the time Otto had been having a Sydney affair with Sal, Otto usually stayed in a squalid little Darlinghurst flatette which he rented but hated. So, quite often, he slept on the couches and floors of friends he had spent the night drinking with.

So, on this Thursday night, the night before Iris and Phillip were having dinner in the Mexican restaurant, Otto, at the invitation of Iris whose house in Annandale he had crashed at sometimes before when he was drunk, went back to her flat. It turned out that they sat up for hours and drank Scotch and talked. (Otto and Sal had recently had a half million dollar bet about a theory of aesthetics and Otto had wanted Iris to be the adjudicator, but Iris was explaining that no-one could adjudicate about the aesthetics of late twentieth century art until the late twenty-first century.) And so at five in the morning Iris couldn't be bothered making up the couch for Otto and said, You can sleep in my bed, it's easier, but we are not going to fuck because I am in love with Phillip.

So, she explained all this to Phillip and he didn't believe that they had slept in the same bed without sex. No-one, he said, could. She said, what if I had slept in the same bed with Sal, or with Peg, or with Jenny, because we were too pissed to make up the couch, you wouldn't be jealous then, and that's how it is with Otto. He agreed that he wouldn't mind about women being in bed with her, but it was a different thing having a man in the bed. She said that just because he couldn't sleep in a bed with a woman and not fuck her didn't mean that other men couldn't, and he said a man who could do that couldn't be much of a man, and she said, are you accusing Otto of being a poofter, and he said no. Which came back to the same thing, that he thought they had had a fuck. But after a while he said he would forgive her, and she said she didn't want to be forgiven for something she hadn't done. As the evening wore on, though, he began to believe her in a sort of a way. He just kept looking at her sideways with a sardonic look on his face and saying something in Greek (which she found out means 'who cares'), because he had once lived in Greece for a year

9

trying to overthrow the Junta.

When they returned to Iris's house they had a nightcap and went to bed. But there was still a definite tension between them and they didn't touch, and after ten minutes Phillip got up and said he had better go home. He said it was no good and that it would always be like this: Iris crashing into bed all the time with drunken journalists when he wasn't around and that he'd had enough of it; that he'd been badly hurt by women in the past and he wasn't staying around to take more of it. Iris pleaded and pleaded with him to stay, and he did. The next morning they made love and all the bad things they had talked about in the evening were forgotten.

They were having breakfast quietly and reading things to each other from the Saturday papers when Sal arrived. It had been arranged that Sal would pick up Iris to accompany her to the auction sale of her house. She didn't want to be alone when she sold it. She needed to sell it so that she could look after the children and pay off her credit cards, and she knew Robert, her ex-husband who was overseas with his new girlfriend, would say that she had mismanaged her money.

'How did last night go?' Iris asked Sal before she had even sat down.

Sal pulled one of those faces, eyes askew and mouth grimacing downwards, that she pulls when she's trying to be funny about something she doesn't think is a bit funny. 'Oh, I don't know,' she shrugged, 'I think it's fucking up.'

She was talking about the evening spent with Tony again last night. Their fifth evening in a row. She had looked forward to it all during the day and had bought new perfume – well, a new bottle of Rive Gauche which was the perfume she always wore because she believed in constancy and stability – and new black nail polish and put a pink stripe in her hair.

'Don't be silly, Sal. He's crackers about you. I can tell.'

Phillip was looking bored. Bloody girls' talk, if you could call them girls. And he wanted to spend breakfast alone with Iris after the problems of the night before, to consolidate things. And he didn't have time to waste sitting around the kitchen listening to this kind of gossip when his typewriter was sitting at home in his Kings Cross flat with a blank reproachful sheet of paper in it, because Phillip was, among other things, a distinguished and famous writer. And he had his Saturday morning routines to get through before he got to the typewriter, which, along with other chores this morning, consisted of going to the laundromat and washing seven of his twenty-two drip-dry shirts because although it was only November he was already through all of them whereas usually he could get by half of summer or at least till Christmas without washing any of them, but now his routine was getting fucked up because of always having to take Iris to restaurants and wearing clean shirts.

'Well, I don't think he's crackers about me any more.'

'Of course he is.'

'No, Iris, this is different. We had a good night to begin with. He bought me flowers, November lilies, white, and he took me to Claude's and then back at home we drank Moet et Chandon in bed and he told me he thought he loved me, but then bloody Otto turned up at midnight and bloody Leo let him in and of course he came straight into the bedroom, but luckily Tony had fallen asleep by then, so I made a "shush" sign to Otto and pushed him into the lounge-room . . .'

Phillip stopped looking bored.

'*Your* Otto?' he said to Iris. 'You mean he was here on Thursday and at Sal's last night?'

Iris tried to be patient. 'Well no. But yes, the Otto who was here on Thursday night, but really he's *Sal's* Otto.' She turned to Sal.

11

'We had a few problems last night too. Because of Otto, too. When you were out with Tony on Thursday night, he crashed here, actually in my bed, but just as friends, you know, he was really drunk, well so was I probably, but Phillip doesn't understand and got pissed off and . . .'

Sal looked puzzled. 'So what, Otto's done that before hasn't he?'

Phillip looked puzzled. Iris ignored him. 'And then what happened?'

'Well I stayed up and Otto and I drank a bottle of the Moet Tony bought and we talked and I did try to explain things, but Otto was a bit drunk and didn't seem to care and just kept going on about his bloody theory of aesthetics, as if I care about Leavis and Raymond Williams and Derrida and whoever else he was raving about. Then eventually he left. And when I got back into bed Tony had woken up and wanted to know where I had been, so I had to tell him about Otto and how although I was very fond of him, Otto that is, it wasn't anything really *important* and how in any case he has a wife and children and only spends a couple of nights a week in Sydney when he sometimes sees me – usually, anyway – and I'm sorry, Phillip, that you're pissed off about Otto coming here, but it's not Iris's fault, it's mine for being out with Tony that night but I can't help it because I love him. Anyway all that candid confession was a bummer because it made Tony tell me about his Melbourne girlfriend, and how his relationship, God I hate that word, with me is really all a bit too *difficult* – which is a load of bullshit because before Otto arrived he'd been raving on about how he loved me or thought he did. Well he must have had a big re-think while I was drinking with Otto, a big agonising re-a-fucking-praisal, because suddenly it's all too difficult. Then he got really quiet and went to sleep, this was about four o'clock, and he was still quiet this morning, and he left and said I was a very good person, *good*

12

mind you, and how he'd like to stay friends and could we have dinner tomorrow night.'

Sal sighed.

'There's no point in having dinner with him when he just wants to stay friends. Oh fuck fuck fuck *fuck*.' She banged her fists on the table. 'Fuck, I hate love.' Tears came to her eyes. 'Peg's right,' she said. 'There ought to be a drug we can take to kill our hormones when they get into a lather.'

Phillip told her that he thought it mightn't be a bad idea to stay friends with him for the time being, it was better than nothing, and things might eventually improve. Sal told him fuck that, she wanted the sex and the romance and the love bits too.

Phillip was smiling. He felt somehow comforted by the fact that Otto's visit to Sydney was wreaking havoc in more households than one. He felt a quiet solidarity with Tony.

'And what's probably nearly as bad,' said Sal, her head in her arms on the table, 'I've probably lost Otto too now. No love, no friendly sex. And it was all going so well. Why can't men keep more than one idea in their heads at a bloody time. So what does it matter about Tony's girlfriend. I told him we could still be Sydney lovers, that I would never cause any problems, that I would never embarrass him, that I wouldn't ring him at home, but no, he said, it's too *difficult*.'

Iris said, 'She's probably really awful.'

'Who?'

'The Melbourne girlfriend. Harry probably knows who she is, he's bound to. I could find out about her. Harry's always very chivalrous about things like that, about saying that women we don't want to like are awful. He'll even say they're ugly.'

Phillip touched Iris's hand and smiled. 'You two are going to miss the auction if you don't get going.'

'That'd be right,' Sal groaned. 'No love, no casual sex,

13

no bloody money, and then Robert'll come back and take the kids off me because I'm too slack to sell the house. Oh God. *Fuck*.' Tears came to her eyes again. 'And what's more,' she yelled at Iris whose hand was still being touched by Phillip, 'I *hate* people who are in love. They make me want to *spew*.' Her head slumped down on the table again.

'Come on Sal, we'd better go. It'll work out. Tony will work out that he can't stand to be without you. And Otto will come back. Ring him at the paper next week.'

'Oh I'm having lunch with him today at the Malaya. Will you come too, Iris? I won't be able to cope, not on my own. And he's so hurt about last night, not that he has any right to be, but he is.'

Iris said she would, and Phillip asked if Sal would give him a lift to the bus stop. So they all got into Sal's car with Iris in the back, and when she put her arm around Phillip's neck in the front seat, Sal yelled at her again. 'I *hate* people who are happy, they make me *sick*.'

And they dropped Phillip in Parramatta Road, and Sal cried all the way to the auction with Iris's arm around her.

Colour Him Gone

Jean Bedford

He rings in the early afternoon. It is only two hours since he has last rung, four hours since she has seen him.

'How are you?' he asks.

'Pretty much the same.'

'Yeah.' His voice is soft; in the background she can hear a radio, phones, people – men – talking and laughing. She is reminded of her friend Yves, and how he said once, 'Never talk seriously to lovers on the phone. For all you know they're pointing at the handset and laughing silently at what you say.' He had mimed an outrageous grimace at an imaginary phone.

'What are you laughing at?'

'Nothing,' she says. 'How's it going?'

'Good.' There are silences when they talk on the telephone. 'I'll be finished soon, I think.'

Together they say 'What about a drink?'

'I'll come over,' he says. 'Then I've got to go to that dinner, but I'll come back later.'

'OK.'

She showers, quickly. She has been walking round in her dressing-gown, in a daze, since he left this morning. She doesn't think – he's coming over now. She doesn't think at all. This is all feeling, no thought yet. This is still nerve-endings, a husk in the voice, the jolt somewhere

15

behind the ribs when they touch, accidentally or deliberately. This is still lying wound around each other in
sleep, responding in sleep to the slightest shift or stirring.
If she thought, she would think – this is being in love.
But she is too far in to think.

'Tony?' says Leo, seeing her painting black around her
eyes in the bathroom.

'Yep. He's coming over now.'

Leo watches her wide eyes in the mirror and makes a
face and hugs her from behind.

'Jealous,' she says.

'Ha!' Leo says.

The children are home from school when Tony ar-
rives, a gang of them, Maria and Rosie and their friends
Hannah and Rebel. Maria has her witches' Tarot spread
out on the kitchen table. She calls out to him –

'Tony! Let me read your Tarot. Do you dare?'

'Let him get in the door,' Sal says. She kisses him and
they hold each other.

'I've brought you a present,' he says. There is champagne under his arm, too. 'It's not wrapped, sorry.'

She laughs. It is a tape of a group he was talking about
yesterday. She is touched, really moved. Her boyfriends
seldom give her presents, except flowers and champagne,
which of course do not last long. Though Alec had given
her a silk scarf, and that peculiar electric kettle. God, my
mind wanders, she thinks. She mumbles thanks, she is
blushing, smiling.

He opens the champagne and pours large glasses, the
flower-frosted quarter-bottle glasses that she has already
chilled.

'Tony? Come on. Madame Maria will tell your future.
Your past. Your present even.' The girls snicker. They
think it is hilarious that their mother is in love.

He sits down with them patiently. Sal stands behind

16

him with her fingers resting on his neck and he puts his hand back to hold hers. She presses herself against him. He leans his head into her breast.

His significator, the girls decide, is the King of Swords. A dark man, his sword over his left shoulder, on his shield a crown. Sal knows what her own Tarot makes of this character: he is justice, military or political. He has the power of life and death; and reversed he is cruelty, perversity, a man of evil intentions. The sinister Aleister Crowley says he is the destroyer, unstable and untrustworthy, impossible to get a grip on . . . Maria's pack is more benign: a man of worldly power. The girls agree that this is Tony. They are giggling, setting out the cards – the adults' happiness infects them. They read the most romantic meanings – a new, wonderful, relationship; the death of the old way of life, the birth of the new.

'That's Mummy,' says Maria triumphantly, turning up the Queen of Cups. It is Sal's significator when she plays with her own set.

'See,' says Maria. 'A wise woman, mature and generous. Loving, tolerant, benef, benif . . .'

'Benificent. That's me,' Sal says. She and Tony laugh into each other. He holds her hand hard.

'Yeah,' Hannah is excited. 'See. It all works out. *You* fall in love with *Sal*, and . . .'

'Cut the social work,' Sal says, not laughing now, 'and read the cards.'

'Cut the cards and read the social work,' says Maria, trying out her wit.

But Sal has had enough and she tells the kids to piss off, that she and Tony want to talk. They go, giggling: 'Yeah, *talk*! We know . . .'

She smiles at him, they kiss; but looking back she will wonder if that wasn't perhaps when she felt the first faint flutters of the goosesteps . . .

When he goes she walks with him to the corner; she is meeting Harry and Iris at the wine bar. They walk together like one person, they stop to stare at each other, to drink each other's mouths. He gets into the taxi and says he will see her after his dinner.

'Where's your *petit ami*?' says Harry.

'I've put it in a taxi,' she says. 'But I'll get it back later.' She and Iris smile at each other.

Dusty Springfield blares out into the hot morning: 'Wear your hair, Just for him. Do the things, He likes to do – oo . . .' Leo and his new friend Vince, who Sal keeps calling Wayne, their generic term for Leo's casual friends, are sitting with the kids at breakfast. Tony stands uncertainly, waiting for Sal to kiss him at the door. There has been a shift, she can sense it already. They are to meet for lunch, one of Harry's lunches, but she has a vague feeling that perhaps she shouldn't go. She kisses him, she has not yet washed his sperm from her mouth, she likes its acrid aftertaste. She wonders if he does.

'I'll ring you later in the morning,' he says.

'No, I won't be here. I'll ring you.' She thinks she really should not go to the lunch, but she can't think why not.

'Amazing,' says Jilly, at their script meeting. 'Only a few weeks ago you were saying you didn't think you could do it again . . .'

'I know.' Sal has been there an hour and they have drunk coffee and talked, not about Jilly's script, but about love. They have been analysing it, the way women do together, weaving their own histories, point and counterpoint, like a piece of highly satisfying music.

'I have to ring him now,' Sal says. She is smug, and Jilly understands. Jilly, they have decided long ago, is the

18

one single factor that caused Sal and Robert to split up two years ago after eleven years of marriage. If only Jilly had come to that dinner in London, if she hadn't been flying out to Switzerland in the morning, Sal would not have stayed with David that night, they would not have had their torrid holiday affair, she would not have told Robert about it, he would not, in Sal's words, have gone right up the chimney. Perhaps they would still be together. Sometimes Sal wonders if that would have been better. She and Jilly have talked about this, too, this morning. Their themes are often repetitive, like all good music; there are minor keys, variations, trills and flourishes. *Lento*, *presto*, *piano*, *forte*. Women make this music out of their daily lives, their emotions, their shrewd understanding. Women colour themselves in, and their friends and their lovers, endlessly; women make their reality of the subtlest shades of colour and sound.

Sal rings Tony, and even over the phone she feels his withdrawal. She is puzzled, but she and Jilly work on the script and they finish in time, so she decides she will go to lunch. After all, her publisher will be there and she hasn't seen him for a long time. She is fond of him, she would go whether Tony was there or not. She thinks she will suggest that Tony go back to where he is officially staying tonight, some space might be a good idea.

But in the end, when she does suggest this, he will say no, he wants to be with her. So how will she cope with the confusion, later, when he tells her they will have to cool it? How will she be able to help blaming her own clumsiness, Otto's arrival that night, at midnight? Something, she will think, there must be some *reason*, I must have done something wrong. Then she will think, no, he is an honourable man, he is being honest about *his* life, he just can't hack it.

These melodies will intertwine in the next weeks, there will creep in sour notes, diminished sevenths. She will not have Dusty's trumpets to usher in a plaintive simple tune, the chords will become confused, jangling, before she and her women friends have gone over it enough to arrive at the final muted cadences and she finds some peace again.

Leo and the children sit eating their cornflakes. Sal has gone back to bed with a cup of tea.

'I really liked Tony,' Maria says, with her mouth full.

'I liked Tony as well,' says Rosie. She wouldn't have thought of it for herself.

'Yes, so did I,' says Leo. They sit in silence for a while.

'Mummy liked him too.' Maria at eleven understands these things. 'I think she's got a broken heart.'

'Eat your cornflakes,' Leo says.

'Mum? *Have* you got a broken heart?' Maria asks Sal in the kitchen at lunchtime.

'Ye – es!' Sal wails and clutches her and they stand hugging and laughing over the peanut butter sandwiches. Sal wants Maria to dance to the beat of a very different drum.

The Night They Planned Iris's Wedding

Jean Bedford

Sal was in a foul mood. Robert had been back in town for two days and already, she said to Iris, she was having deep anxiety symptoms. After seeing him two days in a row she was falling, she said, into the black hole. She lay on her bed all through the second afternoon, after Robert had gone, telling herself she would *not* fall into the black hole. Fuck it, she thought, my life's nothing but a series of having to be *friends* with people, whether I love them, or hate them, or both or neither.

Her mood was not helped by Tony ringing to make dinner arrangements. Things between them were already going wrong – there had been the night Otto arrived at midnight and Sal had had to get out of bed to talk to him and had ended up drinking all the champagne Tony had brought, for a start, and Tony had already said once or twice in this previous week that he thought they were seeing too much of each other, that perhaps they should cool it a little. So when he rang she was flustered. She'd meant to convey something with this phone call, but, still thinking about Robert, she didn't remember what she'd meant to convey.

'At least,' she said to Iris later, 'I hung up first.' But she'd also crawled back into bed with her Arthurian romance, thinking – it's all fucked. She'd been obsessed with this statement lately, it was coming to seem a most elegant summation. This time last week, she thought, Tony was ringing to say he was knocking off early and he'd come round for a drink before his official dinner. This time last week . . . Athena Starwoman in the *Mirror* had told her she'd be on cloud nine, and she was. She heaved herself off the bed and went to see if Spiro, her other house-mate, had bought the paper. Spiro was unable to get through the day without reading his stars, too. The paper was under the ginger cat on the kitchen bench, but her stars were boring: a partial eclipse of the sun and the new moon in Scorpio, a most unreliable sign. Athena said to put everything off. Tony's stars said that problems would be resolved after the weekend. Sal wished she hadn't agreed to dinner on Friday.

She went back to bed. Robert had the kids and she had stacks of work she wasn't doing. She put her book down and tried to think, but thoughts wouldn't come. The phone rang.

'Hi. Sal?' It was Iris.

'How'd it go?' Sal asked. Iris had been to see Sal's (and Robert's) truly amazing accountant.

'Wonderful. Everything's OK. Come and have a drink.'

'Well, why not?'

She went to comb her hair and the phone rang again. Leo and Spiro were playing chess in the living-room so Sal answered it.

'It's me again,' said Iris.

'Yeah?'

'I forgot to tell you we're technically corporate conspirators. Ken said we've done what Harry M. got five years for.'

'Oh shit.'

'He says you'd better see him.'

They were both laughing so much Sal hardly heard her.

'OK, I will. I'll ring him tomorrow.'

Peg, who shared Iris's house, arrived at the wine bar after a while, and Sal had to bring her up to date on all the stuff Iris already knew. Peg was nearly as upset as she thought Sal had been. She'd kept saying how brave Sal was, even to think of falling in love. Sal was beginning to think it had been a recurrence of a chronic stupidity.

'And I suppose you and Phillip are still *happy*?' Sal said bitterly to Iris. She knew they'd been away during the week.

'Yes, very,' Iris said, but her voice was troubled. She explained: 'I think he wants us to get married, and I won't do that.'

Sal looked at Peg.

'Yes!' they said together. 'Get married. What a wedding!'

Iris laughed.

'No, Iris,' Sal said. 'You don't have to live with him or change your name, people don't these days. But the wedding! Imagine it! No-one's been married for ages.'

They did begin to imagine it until they were all crying with laughter. Peg and Sal were to be matrons-of-honour in mauve guipure lace over white satin. Peg described the dresses – strapless, boned, a fish-tail pleat, chiffon shoulder slips. Old friends of Iris's, Jenny and Dianna, neither of whom had ever married, would be bridesmaids, in reverse colours. Sal's daughters and all their friends would be flower-girls and carry baskets of roses. The ceremony was to be in the derros' park outside Kinselas – they'd take over the restaurant for the reception. Harry would give Iris away, Phillip would have a famous and awful communist writer as best man. The colour scheme throughout would be mauve and yellow. Cabbage roses featured prominently. Leo and Ariel would write the Epithalamium, a four-hour epic in medieval Latin (Leo

23

had done a classics degree) and Old Norse, (Ariel, a thriller-writer and one of Sal's closest friends, had studied Icelandic languages once). There would be choruses which all the guests would be required to chant.

'I want to wear a yellow going-away suit,' Iris said. 'With a waist and a peplum and a pleat. And very high yellow shoes.'

'And a pill-box hat,' said Peg, her eyes very round.

'And Harry's suit has to be mauve,' said Sal.

'Absolutely,' Peg said, 'with a purple Liberty tie.'

'We'll all smoke all through the ceremony.' Iris was remembering Jenny graduating in Arts at the age of fifty-seven – the photos showed them all smiling, cigarettes dangling from every hand.

'Can we have picture hats?' Sal asked Peg.

'Absolutely. As long as they're covered in cabbage roses.'

'I want a dress like Lady Di's,' said Iris.

'Of course,' said Peg, like the Fairy Godmother. 'And Phillip should be all in white with mauve-tinted sunglasses.'

Sal looked worried. 'Do you think he'll come at it?'

'It doesn't matter,' Peg said. 'Anyone'll do at this stage.'

Louise at the wine bar said they'd turn on the shower tea and that the cigarette companies would probably sponsor the whole thing. That got Sal and Iris enthused about who should have the television rights.

'It could be a series,' Sal said.

Eventually they left, and Sal walked home thinking that women together, laughing, could apparently heal anything. She fell into bed with hardly a thought of the next night, Friday.

On Saturday morning Sal burst into Iris's kitchen. Phillip was there and he and Iris were having breakfast.

'How's it going?' Iris said. She knew that Sal had been anxious about the dinner date last night.

Phillip looked slightly annoyed – this was the second Saturday in a row Sal had interrupted his papers and bacon and eggs with Iris. He was clearly wondering if it was going to become a habit.

'It's truly fucked now,' Sal said savagely. 'It's the *friends* routine again, only this time he means it. We're not even going to *see* each other for the rest of the time he's here because he can't trust himself to stick to it. I'm some sort of Delilah figure or Devil Woman or something . . .'

Phillip had a funny look on his face, almost as if that idea struck a chord somewhere. Iris glared at him and he turned sympathetically to Sal.

'Perhaps he's jealous,' he suggested, 'Otto turning up last week . . .'

'No,' Sal dismissed that with a grimace. 'It's all about *him*, what *he* can and can't cope with . . . *Bloody* men!'

She sat down and began to pick absently at Iris's bacon rind. Iris poured her a cup of tea and she drank it without appearing to notice. Iris sighed.

'Sal,' she said. 'We're thinking of going to Bondi for the day. Do you want to come?'

'Nah,' Sal said, then, 'sorry, thanks, but no I can't. The kids are coming back to my place for the weekend while Robert gets himself settled in again. But I'll drive you to the train if you like.'

On the way, Sal told Iris and Phillip that if they didn't stop holding hands over the back of the seat they could walk.

The election was the next weekend and Sal watched it on television at the coast house with Mary.

'What happened to Tony?' Mary asked. Mary was pissed off – she had had to vote for a local right wing independent in order to prevent an even worse Labor candidate getting in.

'He's back in Melbourne, probably,' Sal said. She half expected to see him on the screen when they showed the counting and the politicians crowding in the Party rooms.

Mary looked at her but said nothing. She understood, there was no call for her famous acerbic comments here. Sal was grateful – Mary's marriage had broken up at around the same time as hers, in fact Mary's husband Jack blamed Sal for it. It had provided a bad example, he said. She looked around the large room that she and Robert had designed from the derelict shell they had bought years ago and gave a shiver.

'What's the matter?'

'Nothing – just, lots of ghosts here.' She laughed. She had told Mary why Robert wouldn't use this house any more – 'Too many ghosts and bad memories,' he had said and she had been deeply hurt, because some of the memories were good and there were benign ghosts, too, from the years they had lived here. It had been a hospitable house – always food in the fridge for Sydney friends en route to somewhere else or locals who dropped in; regular Sunday lunches with city people who enjoyed the charming train trip or the drive through the park. She had not wanted to move back to Sydney, nor had the children. She had a flash of resentment that she had given in for Robert's convenience. Then she thought, No, I would have gone mad here that first year, on my own.

Now, there were new ghosts – Tony, waking in the afternoon from the mattress in Maria's old room (because Leo wouldn't give up what he called the master bedroom), reaching for her, already dressed and distracted because she had to make the girls their dinner. Tony, at the beach, and their starfish competition. Tony, sitting in the chair Mary sat in now, telling her about his first marriage, about how he had come to work in party politics. Tony, tentatively teasing her daughters, winning their approval. She thought she could see what Robert had meant.

'Come on. Don't get maudlin on me,' Mary said. 'This shit,' she gestured at the television, 'this is enough to cause a deep depression. Who needs *lurv* when you can get angry about politics?'

Later, when Mary had gone, Sal moved around the large house turning off the lights. She had drunk a great deal of wine, and she sat on the bed in the spare room that Robert had sometimes used during their increasing periods of separate coldness. But sometimes, she thought, sometimes I crept down here and we were happy for the night. She wondered if she would ever work out what had been *her* mistakes, and what had been unavoidable.

Epithalamium

Rosemary Creswell

It was after Sal and Peg planned Iris's wedding that things between Iris and Phillip really went wrong.

Iris and Sal and Peg were idling away a few hours at the wine bar one night. Iris and Sal had been idling away the afternoon at the wine bar since lunchtime and Peg had joined them on her way home from visiting a spiritualist. Peg was writing another book and they were discussing whether the narrative should be in the first or third person.

'The first, I reckon,' said Sal whose own books were a mixture of persons.

'The trouble with that,' said Peg, 'is that I always get it muddled up with myself.'

'Who *is* talking?' asked Iris.

'Well, I don't know. I'm writing this book backwards. I know what she does, but I don't know who she is because I'm not up to the first chapter, which is last, in my head.'

Iris talked about that not mattering and people being defined by their action and not having any central persona which she vaguely remembered from first year philosophy twenty-five years ago but she couldn't remember which philosopher.

None of them could remember anything much that

week. They were having a lot of trouble with nouns, especially proper ones. Only that morning Iris had needed to look up something in the *Shorter O.E.D.* but couldn't find the dictionary. She had asked Peg, who lived with her, if she had been using it and Peg had said no. But later when Peg was making her bed she had found one of each volume under her pillows as though the words were going to seep into her head in the night.

They worried about this failure to remember substantives. Peg, who was a nursing sister, referred to the problem as dealing only in connective tissue not with muscle and bones. Sal said it was caused by drinking but as Iris pointed out only she and Sal drank a lot, not Peg, but Peg had just the same problem. Iris was annoyed that Sal said it was drinking.

Sal then thought it was the full moon.

'Well, even if I don't quite know who I'm writing about, she's got to have a certain age and appearance and so on, and a name I suppose.'

'That's immaterial,' said Sal.

'As a matter of fact it's very material,' Peg snapped. She was having trouble with this book.

Iris tried to explain the doctrine of Nominalism to them – she was in a philosophical frame of mind – but she couldn't remember much about that either.

They were silent for a while and Iris squeaked the wine glass by running her finger around the rim.

'Phillip asked me to marry him last night,' she said.

'What,' Sal screamed, animated, leaning forward. 'Why didn't you tell us before?'

'I forgot.'

'You forgot! You mean we've been here seven hours and you've only just remembered?'

'When is it?' asked Peg.

'Oh I'm not going to. It was just drunken talk at five a.m., but even if it was sober I'd have said no.'

'You will say yes,' said Sal. 'You are going to get

29

married. It's your duty. We need an uplifting human emotional event for 1985 and your marriage will be it. All of Sydney needs an uplifting event for the rest of this century and your wedding is it.'

Peg agreed. 'Absolutely,' she said. 'All of Australia. Don't be selfish.'

'Harry will give you away,' said Sal, 'he likes ceremonies and Peg and I will be the bridesmaids, no I mean matrons-of-honour.'

'And Jenny and Dianna will be bridesmaids,' said Peg, 'because they are nearly sixty and will enjoy it.'

Sal said it should be colour co-ordinated and thought of red because Phillip was left wing.

Peg felt that was too garish for such a subtle event, and such a significant one. 'Harry should wear a mauve suit,' she said, 'and Phillip will wear a mauve shirt and tie with a white suit. White for peace.'

'And mauve lace over white satin for us,' said Sal. 'And bonnets, mauve bonnets.'

Peg thought matrons-of-honour shouldn't wear bonnets.

'Big crownless picture hats is what we'll have,' she said.

'With mauve cabbage roses on them,' said Sal.

'And sweetheart necklines,' said Peg.

'And white lace over mauve satin for the bridesmaids,' said Sal.

(Later, when they explained the colour scheme to Jenny, Jenny said she wanted pink. Sal got annoyed with her for wrecking the co-ordination but Peg said it was alright, Jenny and Ida could have pink tulle kick pleats in their mauve and white dresses.)

'And in the derros' park opposite Kinselas with the reception in Kinselas,' Sal went on.

'Absolutely,' said Peg. 'With the honeymoon at the Marxist Summer School.'

'Yellow for your going-away outfit,' said Sal. 'Mauve

30

and yellow and white will be the colours, with a dash of pink for the bridesmaids.'

'A lemon linen suit with a pill box hat and a half veil,' said Peg.

'Mauve and yellow and white with a dash of pink will become the fashion colours of the decade,' said Sal. 'Jenny Kee jumpers, Maggie T. shirts, Prue Acton dresses, Stuart Membery jackets. We'll patent the colour combo.'

'And lemon patent-leather high-heel court shoes,' said Peg.

'And Leo and Ariel will write a long epithalamium,' said Sal, 'which will be read at the reception. With rhyming couplets in Old Norse at the end of each verse which will be recited by the guests.'

Peg felt this would take some of the spontaneity out of things, but Sal explained that great events have to be planned or they get out of hand, so Peg said, 'Absolutely.'

'Don't just sit there Iris,' yelled Sal. 'Take notes or something. It's going to happen and these things have to be prepared and co-ordinated.'

Iris was embarrassed. It was getting out of hand. Even though Phillip had been drunk and it was a silly idea, it was a gesture of love. And she did love him. She explained this to them.

'We're not knocking it, Iris,' said Sal. 'We're celebrating love in the last fifth of the twentieth century. We are giving thanks to love in a loveless world.'

'I think Phillip's very brave saying that,' said Peg. 'I mean I don't mean brave because he said it to *you*, not brave because he wants to marry *you*, just brave for saying it. Like a knight in the middle ages or something.'

'Yes, courtly,' agreed Sal. 'He's courtly. *Fin amour.*'

And gradually Iris was drawn into it and they planned it over four bottles of Dom Perignon which Sal couldn't afford but which she bought on her Bankcard because she

31

said it was worth it. And they laughed a lot and in the end all the customers in the wine bar were drawn in and Louise the proprietor wanted exclusive rights on catering for the shower and kitchen teas, and the guitarist wanted to be a troubador at the wedding reception and Peg said there should be ten, and Louise said Marlboro could sponsor it, and Peg wanted to organise the sale of the film rights and Sal said she would write the book of the film. It was a great night.

It had all seemed very funny at the time, but when Iris told Phillip he was not amused. He was much more than not amused. He was very angry.

It was the following night and they were at the movies, *The Big Chill*. Iris tried to explain that they had not been mocking his emotions, they had been celebrating them. It had been a eulogy to love between a man and a woman. An epithalamium, a *chanson d'amour*. A testament to his honest courage. A paean to the institution of marriage in the twentieth century.

He was unconvinced and angry. He told Iris he would never ever reveal his emotions to her again. He said that she and her women friends were dedicated to trivialising all male feelings. That they were interested only in drinking and the emasculation of men. That they didn't deserve love. That it was no wonder Sal's and Peg's husbands had divorced them years ago. That it didn't surprise him that no-one had ever married her.

No matter how hard Iris tried to defend the planning of the wedding it just made things worse.

She felt wretched.

Alone in bed that night, she wondered if she shouldn't have said yes.

At The Round Table

Rosemary Creswell

The last time Iris was in New York, which was the first time, no-one at the Algonquin Hotel had spoken to her. She had had no adventures, let alone any sexual ones. Not that she was staying at the Algonquin, it was too expensive. But she had gone there late one night, drenched from the rain and sat there over two Heinekens because she didn't know what else to order or whether she could pronounce or afford whatever else they sold. She had been told that the Blue Bar was the most sociable bar in the world and had imagined that lots of people would welcome her, from Australia and first time in New York, but instead they ignored her or looked at her dismissively as though she were an elderly and rather poorly dressed hooker.

This time, a year later, she thought things would be better. She was better equipped for New York. So, after twenty-four hours of flying and nearly sixty hours of no sleep, she checked in at ten p.m. into the Royalton Hotel across the road and then walked over to the Blue Bar. The tiny bar was crowded with men, most of them in suits, except for a woman sitting on a stool at one end of the bar. This woman was very drunk. Iris sat down at the only vacant table, a small round table in the corner and next to the bar. Iris smiled to herself. It wasn't *the* Round Table, but it was the Algonquin, and she was happy.

33

Iris again ordered a Heineken, worked out the fifteen
percent tip, and did some mental sums to calculate how
many drinks per night for fifteen nights she could have.
She wondered if, in this bar, it would be more correct to
pay twenty percent. She felt she looked right. She was
wearing long boots, a grey woollen jumper, a long black
skirt and long colourful beads. Her hair was a bit messed
from the sleepless hours of flying, but she had wet it in
her hotel and puffed it up a bit with the dryer. And she
had put new makeup on. She also had a brown leather
Italian handbag and a brown leather briefcase. Her friend
Ernest had once written that when in bars and restaurants
alone, it is better to be reading a book, writing a manu-
script, or most preferable of all, typing at a typewriter, so
as not to seem too lonely or expectant. She smiled again
as she realised that on this round table a typewriter would
hardly fit. She felt, however, that her briefcase was suf-
ficient to establish her independent and professional
status. In addition, to stave off any possible misconstruc-
tion from the men in the bar that she might be lonely, she
had bought New York postcards at the airport and
busied herself writing them to Peg and Sal and Jenny to
make them envious. 'At the Blue Bar in the Algonquin,'
she started each of them. She had also chosen a large card
of Ronald and Nancy Reagan to send to Phillip as a joke
because he regarded them as The Enemy.

Occupied like this, she was startled when the woman
on the stool next to her table began to speak loudly to
her. She was well-dressed in a suit and silk scarf and she
was older than Iris. She was even drunker than Iris had at
first thought. She said her name was Renata. She explained to Iris that she was finishing a B.A. degree at
Fordham University on West 60th Street, and the following day, as her final assignment, had to give a paper on
Bernini's *Daphne and Apollo*. To prove this, she opened
her large handbag and showed Iris all her research and
photocopying on the subject. She also explained that the

reason she was drinking wine was that she had been drinking martinis all night but the barman refused to serve her any more so she was reduced to red wine. Iris thought this decision of the barman's was a bit illogical. Renata then explained to Iris that she didn't think she would bother to give the paper as she couldn't pay for the fees so she wouldn't get her degree anyway. She smiled,

'I'm an alcoholic,' she said cheerfully, 'and I've spent all my fees on drinks.'

She leant over conspiratorially towards Iris, laughing, and Iris worried that she would fall off her stool.

'Have you noticed,' she asked, 'that women don't like sex? Whenever men want to fuck them, they just turn into trees, just like that,' she said, snapping her fingers, 'just like Daphne.'

She sucked at her nearly empty glass of wine.

'Do you know I've never been pregnant,' she said, 'though I've had plenty of opportunities. Look,' she said, lifting up her fringe and displaying her forehead, 'fifty-nine and no wrinkles.'

She rolled her eyes upwards grotesquely and fluttered her eyelashes at the men in the bar, who had fallen into a kind of hush and were listening to her.

'Once,' she went on, 'when I was young, I met a Scotsman who was a banker and who wanted to fuck me in the Rockefeller Plaza, but I was a bit inhibited and so I pretended that I had somewhere else to go but really it was just back to my room which I shared with another alcoholic girl. As a matter of fact, that's why I drink now, because I don't like the hotel room I live in. Anyway, later he became President of a big merchant bank – that was after I met him. His name was Rory McPhee.' She laughed and knocked over what was left of her wine. 'I suppose he's fat and bald and old now, roaming in the gloaming in the highlands in a kilt.' She laughed again. 'Or more likely paying pretty whores in the south of France.'

Then Renata decided to join Iris at her round table. Iris
bought her another glass of red wine because she knew
how it felt to knock your glass over even if it was nearly
empty. Renata asked Iris what she did and Iris explained
that she was a literary agent from Australia, which was
why she was drinking at the Algonquin. Renata said that
Iris was lucky to have met her because she was a great
writer. Also, she was hoping to go to Australia to meet a
sheep farmer. Also, she was a great dancer and did Iris
handle dancers. She pulled up her skirt and stretched out
a leg and said, 'Better legs than Betty Grable.'

When Iris said she didn't handle dancers, Renata kicked
her in the leg, 'Why have you got your boots on?' she
demanded to know.

Then she asked Iris if Iris herself wrote. When Iris said
no, Renata shouted, 'How can you be a literary agent
when you can't even write?'

She kicked Iris again.

'Cheap Australian boots. It's April in New York. Cheap
Australian boots and your cheap Australian clothes and
your cheap Australian hairdo. And you can't even write.
Call yourself an agent.'

She leered at Iris. Things were turning ugly. Everyone
was listening. Iris was getting scared. She said, 'Look,
I'm very tired and I'm writing to my friend Sal, and I'd
just like to be alone.'

Renata patted her smooth brow and pulled down her
skirt and smoothed it over her knees.

'You're just a cheap Australian literary slut looking for
a fuck in New York because you can't get a sheep farmer
in Australia. You can't write, so you have to fuck.'

She turned to the silent crowd and yelled, 'Any of you
want a fuck because Iris here is after one.'

The barman called the doorman and the doorman es-
corted Renata to the street. She turned to the crowd and
smiled triumphantly as she went.

Iris sat there, petrified as Daphne, staring down at her

briefcase. She wondered whether they were going to throw her out too. She hoped the dim lighting was hiding her flushed face. Thrown out for obscenity on your first night at the Algonquin.

Then a tall large middle-aged man came over. He was a rich banker from Colarado, and he was kind, and he said to Iris, 'That must have been very embarrassing. Can I buy you a drink to show you that New York doesn't usually welcome its visitors that way?' So Iris had a drink with him, a double bourbon which he suggested would be the right drink to recover from the incident.

When she got back to the Royalton, she wrote a long letter to Sal about Renata. She wrote it as a humorous story, but also as a kind of a warning to them. A moral fable. But in the morning she tore it up because it was too depressing and in any case she and Sal could hold their drinks better than Renata.

New York, New York

Rosemary Creswell

Royalton Hotel,
West 44th Street,
New York

Thursday night, 2 May 1985

Dear Sal,

It seems foolish to write to you since I've been phoning
you practically every day, but I'm at a loose end. The
Blue Bar across the road is crowded out and I can't fit
into my usual position on a stool in the corner (usual in
the sense that I've sat on it most of the fourteen nights
I've been here so far); and I don't feel like eating at the
Brazilia again which is the restaurant on West 45th Street
which Harry told me about. Well, Harry couldn't remember its actual address, like all the other good places
and people here he insisted I should visit (sometimes he
couldn't even remember their names, including people),
but I happened to walk past the Brazilia the second day of
my arrival and as it's close I eat there frequently. At first
the Brazilian owner looked at me suspiciously (despite
Harry's assuring me it would be a good place for a woman to eat on her own and drink a couple of bottles of wine

38

without being hassled), but then I told him that an Australian friend of mine who had been in New York recently told me about his restaurant. He at first looked puzzled and then he said, 'Ah yes, you mean Harry with big frizz hair,' and I said yes and from then on he's been very nice to me.

Well, I've been mostly having a good time. Ernest arrived from Europe a few days ago on his way back to Sydney, and it was good to see him, although things didn't quite work out as we'd planned, especially in terms of getting his books published here which is one of the main reasons I came, as you know. I was excited about seeing him because his French publisher has sent me the French reviews of his books which Ernest hasn't seen yet and they say things like 'corrosive humour', 'incisive wit', and they all have very interesting and very French theories about his 'recité' technique. One of the papers devotes half a page to Ernest and half a page to Saul Bellow and Bellow comes off a definite second best! And who but the fucking French could say this: 'We are not the first to discover the Australian novel; even the Australians themselves are beginning to take an interest in it.' Bloody frogs. However, it's all very good for Ernest, and about time he was recognised outside Australia.

Anyway, the first thing that happened was that on Sunday afternoon he left a message at my hotel asking me to ring him at his, which is new and near Grand Central and looks as if it costs about $500 a night, which I later found out it nearly does. So I phoned and he turned up to meet me at the Royalton and I gave him the reviews which I'd had copied down the road at a photocopying place in West 43rd Street which is run by New York blacks dancing to ghetto blasters which means they don't do a very good job and leave pages out, and I had to go back five times to get it done properly. Well, he was naturally very pleased and excited by the reviews which he read in my room over coffee. Actually it was Ernest who told me to stay at the Royalton when I told him I couldn't afford the Algonquin. Ernest told me it would be alright to stay at the Royalton because according to him Ernest Hemingway once wrote a book there. Our Ernest believes you have to have a literary reason for doing everything in New York. His own hotel is so new no-one literary could have yet done anything significant there, but perhaps Ernest believes his stay there will change that. Ernest, mind you, couldn't remember which Hemingway book was written at the Royalton, or when, and no New York literary guide mentions anything about Hemingway ever having stayed there let alone writing a book there, but Ernest swears it's true.

Ernest justifies everything he wants to do in this city by making up something or other about a famous writer having done it, or been there, or drinking there, or living there, or dying there, etc etc etc. He has made up a whole literary geography in his head which contradicts everything written in all the New York literary guides. If you wrote down all of Ernest's made-up literary references you would have a whole alternative literary history of New York. It would confute every PhD thesis ever written on American writers. You would find that all the writers were born in different years to what their biographies say, and you would find them in New York during years in which their biographers claim they were elsewhere, sometimes not even in the United States of America. You would probably find that Henry James was born in England and then went to America later, and vice versa for Wystan Auden. Most likely you would find that Jack London was a teetotaller and that Ralph Waldo Emerson was a drunk. You would probably have Robert Lowell as a small calm man, and Elizabeth Hardwick suffering from uncontrollable mania (though I don't think that Ernest has actually mentioned any women writers). But if he did you would also probably find

40

that Dorothy Parker drank whisky at some oblong table in the White Lion, and that Dylan Thomas died after drinking a martini at the Algonquin. However, Ernest says that a lot of the biographies are wrong, and that it takes a fresh foreign eye to get things right, and that Australians have the best fresh foreign eyes because we have no history or culture ourselves and are therefore not prejudiced by received myth.

I don't suppose it matters, but it's a bit confusing when you're trying to get a literary feel for New York.

Anyway, Ernest suggested we go for a walk and then back to his hotel where we would pick up Thea who was having a rest and hadn't wanted to come on the walk but would have dinner with us later. (Thea is here with Ernest on a business trip for her company and Ernest said she was tired from all her work and that's why she was resting up.)

So Ernest and I stopped in all these bars which Ernest said so-and-so had written a book in. None of them looked to me as if anyone could write a book in them, they were all grubby little affairs with hardly any room and lots of stools squashed close together at narrow bars with noisy people singing Irish songs and things. He also said as we approached them that he knew the barman in each of them, but no-one in them recognised him and then he said that they must have left since he was last in New York. He said that New York is a very mobile city in terms of bar managers. He said it's not like Sydney where staff in restaurants and pubs stay the same for years and years, and you can get free drinks and dinners just by putting their names and their restaurants in your books. In New York they move around a lot, Ernest said, and putting them in your books gets you nowhere anyway because so many American writers put them in their books that the market is over-saturated and they would go broke giving free drinks and meals to hundreds of second-rate writers.

One of the bars Ernest took me to was a very grand bar in a grand hotel attached to Grand Central station by a tunnel which Ernest said all of the writers in the thirties used when they were coming in from out of town to escape their wives. Well, we had a few more drinks there and Ernest told me the reason we were there was because this was the bar where he had picked up a black hooker who had stolen his wallet last time he was in New York. He thought this was something to celebrate. He was drinking toasts to the fact that a black whore had stolen his money. I don't know if he made this up too, but he was very excited about it. It occurred to me that perhaps all the bars we had been to were places where his money had been stolen by prostitutes when he was drunk, and that I was being taken on a guided tour of Ernest-in-the-gutter-in-New-York. The scenes of all his moments of degradation (except he would see them as moments of triumph). You wouldn't exactly think it was something to be proud of, but there you are. You know Ernest, Sal.

Anyway, all this took a few hours and then we arrived at his hotel. Ernest phoned up Thea from the foyer house phone and I heard him say 'What do you mean you don't want to go out?'. Then he said to me that he'd just slip up to the room to freshen up, and he sat me down in the lounge and ordered me a bloody Mary and told me to put it on his account. So I waited and waited and had a few more drinks on his account and then Ernest came down alone. When I asked where Thea was he said she was changing and would be down soon. He muttered about how he always got things wrong with women, he always misread their personalities and moods, and this struck me as probably being true seeing as how it seemed that on his last trip he'd had his money stolen by women in practically every bar he went to.

Anyway, Sal, to cut a long story short, it turned out that he hadn't even told Thea I was in New York or that he was going on a walk with me or that the three of us were meant to be having dinner together. He'd just sprung it on her through the foyer house phone and not surprisingly she was a bit pissed off, not even knowing I was in the country. Not that Ernest and I have been lovers, Sal, well not exactly, but you know, we've known each other for a very long time. Probably he'd taken her on a few walks too, and explained about how many whores had ripped him off. Just the sort of thing to tell your new girlfriend who was seeing the trip as a special occasion between her and you, a shared private journey.

So anyway, Thea made the best of it and was as nice as she could be to me given the fact that Ernest had probably told her they would be having a room-service champagne and oysters and chicken dinner in bed looking out over the New York skyline with a chamber music orchestra playing Gershwin in a corner of their suite.

Ernest said he would take us to the Pen and Pencil. He said this was a famous cartoonists' restaurant where he was well known. He took about an hour to find it, and Thea and I had sore feet in our high heels tramping around while Ernest kept saying 'it's just up this next street' and then pretending he was deliberately taking us the long way to point out more literary famous places, and it turned out to be only about five hundred yards from their hotel after all. It was a small classy place but we were the only people in it the whole night, and Ernest said it must have changed from a dinner to a lunch restaurant since the last time he was in New York. And New York's staff mobility must have affected the Pen and Pencil too, because no-one knew him. The way things had changed in New York since Ernest had last been there, Sal, you'd think he hadn't been there since 1920.

(. . . Hang on Sal, I'm just going down to the foyer – forgot to check at the desk to see if Phillip's been trying to phone me . . . No, no calls as usual. I ring him about six times a day, Sal, and he's only phoned me four times in two weeks. He says it's not necessary to make all these costly calls. It's not as if I'm going to be away all that long. I get into trouble when I phone him for spending so much money. I think he resents the money because the telephone system here is private enterprise. If it was owned by a left wing government he'd probably encourage me to make lots of calls. Give him a ring for me, please, and tell him to phone me and that I'm worth every penny, though by the time you get this letter I'll probably have phoned him another twenty times. I think he's punishing me for being in New York instead of somewhere like Cuba. Tell him I'm going to Nicaragua to join the Sandanista if that makes him happy . . .)

Well, we ate at the Pen and Pencil and when we left Ernest said he'd walk me back to the Royalton, but Thea looked suddenly tired and so he bought me a bunch of tulips instead from Grand Central which I took with me to the Algonquin to have a nightcap. By the way, a funny but awful thing happened on my first night at the Blue Bar, with a woman called Renata, but I'll tell you about it when I get back.

On Tuesday night I had to meet Ernest and Thea again, this time at the Algonquin, where I'd organised for Ernest to meet this editor called Penny from Simon and Schuster, who had read Ernest's work and was enthusiastic about publishing it, and as Ernest was in town it seemed to me a good idea for her to meet him. So I told her I would be with Ernest and a friend of his and we would see her there in the lounge at six. Well Thea and Ernest turned up and we drank in the lounge for an hour or so with me keeping an eye out for this Penny whom I hadn't yet met myself, only written to and talked on the phone. Ernest was peculiarly nervous, talking very loudly and drinking martinis with twists very fast, which was odd I thought seeing how often he deals with publishers in Australia. Well this woman kept walking around the lounge but I didn't think she looked enough like a New York editor to be Penny and also I thought that she would work out that we would be the people she was looking for, if it was her. Then finally I got up and asked if she was Penny and she said yes, so I introduced her and do you know what she said? She said she hadn't thought we were us, because from reading Ernest's work she had assumed his 'friend' would be a man. So it was a bit embarrassing but she sat down and we all talked for a while. Mostly Ernest and Penny talked about films, and after a while she left telling me to phone her the next morning. I thought it was all very successful, but Ernest was oddly gloomy, and we went into the Blue Bar for more drinks.

You see, on previous nights I'd been talking to the manager in the Blue Bar, a man called Brett, and when he found out I was Australian and in publishing, he told me he'd once met an Australian writer in the bar and had read one of his books and liked it, and it turned out to be Ernest when he was last in New York. This was the one time when Ernest didn't seem to be lying about knowing barmen everywhere.

So in we went, and Thea and I sat down and drank while Brett and Ernest met up again, and they talked for hours and hours because it turned out that Brett had been in the SAS in Vietnam and was writing a novel about it, and also it was the subject of the moment because it's the tenth anniversary of America pulling out of Vietnam and tomorrow there's a big veterans' march in New York. (I suppose there's one in Sydney too.)

I heard Ernest telling Brett that he'd been in the Australian SAS too when as you know he was only in National Service decades ago when there were no wars on, and in any case Ernest used to be in moratorium marches, but you know how he's always reading war books and going to military history seminars and going to Verdun and the Middle East and Lone Pine and hanging around

war museums and memorials, so they talked about guns
and parachutes and airlifts and 'Charlie' (I think Ernest
learnt a lot of this from Pat Burgess when he came back
from reporting in Vietnam) and I even heard Ernest say
'the Nam'. At one stage I thought he was going to pull
out his Order of Australia medal and say it was a military
hero's medal. And all this time Thea and I had to just talk
and drink with each other, and with Thea still quite annoyed that I was in New York.

(Well, I'd better go Sal. How's everything? Have you
heard from Tony? Give my love to the girls. Did Sarah
pass her exams? If I were you I'd just send Tony a cheery
postcard just as if you'd suddenly thought of him, accidentally, and was wondering how he was, just in case
he thinks you're pining after him and deliberately not
contacting him because you're sad, which I know you are
but you shouldn't let him know.)

Oh, and I nearly forgot the point. When we left the bar
I told Ernest I'd phone him as soon as I'd phoned Penny
the next morning, and he said he wouldn't go out of his
hotel room until he'd heard from me about Simon and
Schuster. So the next day I rang Penny all ready to go
down and pick up a contract for Ernest to sign, and she
said she'd changed her mind about wanting to publish
him. I was very annoyed and she wouldn't say why, and
I am annoyed because they don't know what they're
missing out on. I had to ring Ernest and tell him, but I
tried to tell him not to worry and that other publishers
would be bidding in auctions for him, but it didn't work
and he was very depressed. He told me I should never
ever again introduce him to publishers because they all
cancel contracts when they've met him no matter how
much they've said they admire his writing, which isn't
true of course. He said he should be kept away from
publishers at all costs. He said he should wear a sign
saying 'publishers keep away', or swing a bell and call
out 'unclean' whenever he was near a publisher. He said

he would never go into literary bars again or to writers' festivals or to literary prize-givings or anywhere where he might run into a publisher. He said he must have some smell which repels publishers.

I tried to cheer him up, but it was no good. I said this was a big city and there were hundreds of publishers who would like him as well as his work, but he said it was just as well he was getting out of town tomorrow to leave me clear to sell his books here without him hampering me by his damaging presence. I felt so sorry for him, Sal, I wanted to rush round to his hotel and hug him.

I ended up telling him that if he wrote up his New York literary guide I would take it straight to the office of Michelin in New York and sell it for millions. He said didn't I know the editorial office of Michelin was in Clermont-Ferrand, and if I'd read *Biggles* I'd know where Clermont-Ferrand was, and what kind of an agent was I if I didn't know elementary things like that, and I said I was only joking and he said his literary map of New York was only a joke too.

So, he's left now Sal, and should be back in Sydney within a day or two, unless he stops over at Honolulu to recover from the setback, so give him a ring to cheer him up if you can. And ask him to show you the French reviews.

I'll probably phone you tomorrow anyway to tell you all this.

Lots of love,
Iris.

No Words

Jean Bedford

Otto and Sal had an unusual relationship, at least in Sal's experience. It had begun thoughtlessly, as these things often do, drunkenly, but it had lasted, apparently aimlessly, but continuing. Sal had shied away from trying to work it out at first.

She had been in one of her rare periods of calm, some weeks after she and Alec had stopped seeing each other, and one afternoon, after a good day's work, she had wandered into Iris's office and found them all drinking in Alec's room – Iris, Alec, Otto and Hope. She had a couple of beers with them and then went down to the wine bar with Iris and Otto. She'd always found Otto attractive, with his big man's grace and hooded eyes, though for years she'd vaguely disliked him for what she took to be arrogance and his dismissal of women. This was the first time she had talked to him at any length and she was surprised at his friendliness. But as he and Iris were pretending to deliberate over whether to order another bottle, she said she had to go, the children were waiting for their dinner.

She fed the kids and had seen them to bed and she and Leo sat in the living-room drinking and reading. She felt, she said to Leo, no pain. 'Weeks of celibacy, no fuck on

48

the horizon, and I really don't care.'

'Bullshit,' said Leo, and she laughed.

The phone rang and Leo answered it.

'It's Iris. She sounds pissed.'

'Hi. Still at the wine bar?'

'No, at home. Otto's here, why don't you come over?'

'Oh,' Sal had been looking forward to bed with the ginger cat and her book. 'Yes, I might, but I'm tired. If I'm not there in half an hour I've gone to sleep.'

Leo told her not to be silly, so she combed her hair and changed her jumper and drove to Iris's house. Alec and Moira were there too, which took her aback a little, but in the end there were just Sal and Otto drinking red wine in Iris's living-room.

'I feel set up,' Sal said, and Otto put his hand on hers.

'I'm staying in Iris's spare room,' he said. He stroked her wrist.

Sal sometimes thought that her fatal flaw was her willingness to be amused. Some Sal inside her shrugged and giggled and thought – Why not?

'OK,' she said, and they kissed.

Some time before dawn, with Otto's sleeping body across hers, she thought she should go home. She thought of Ariel's dingo-job joke, but she couldn't see how she would gnaw her arm off, so she wriggled and edged until she could get out of bed. She arranged some massage-parlour cards around a scrap of paper with her phone number written on it, and crept out. She went home to her sleeping children and stayed up to give them breakfast and get them off to school.

The next week he rang, a couple of days before she had thought he might, and said he was in town. They had dinner and went back to Sal's house and Otto stayed there the next two nights, too.

'I felt like a frightened adolescent, ringing you like that,' Otto said in bed, stroking her back.

'Why?'

'Oh – it was such a clumsy drunken night, and I woke up and you'd gone. Then I saw your phone number and was completely delighted. One of the nicest things that's ever happened to me.'

So it had gone on, for weeks, then months, inarticulate but affectionate, somehow surviving its haphazard nature, often reaching peaks of great sexual pleasure, sometimes consisting of little more than the comfort of friendly bodies sleeping together. And that was plenty, as Sal acknowledged after the years of living without Robert.

But of course, as she said to Iris, and to Ariel, it wasn't entirely satisfactory. There were the times when Sal thought she could let herself fall in love with Otto – the sexual attraction was strong enough, and she liked his mind and his willingness to sit up in bed all night talking, arguing about literary references, and smoking. But, and these days for Sal it was a big but, he had a wife and young child.

'Well, if it wasn't you, it'd be someone else,' Iris said. 'Look at it this way: she should be grateful it's you and not some grasping female who wants to take him away.'

'Yeah. But after all the things I said about Faith when Robert and I were splitting up . . .' She'd ranted then about Faith's selfishness and desperate grasping of Robert.

'Completely different,' Iris said definitely. 'Not the same at all.'

So Sal convinced herself that as long as it remained time out, time Otto spent away from his family anyway, time that she never demanded or seemed to seek, time that she never analysed the meaning of, then it was alright.

Except that it wasn't, still, quite alright. Sal had never

before denied herself the luxury of talking everything out, working through all the emotions at the time. She found this stultifying, in the end. She had never really believed anything that could not be put into endless words: if she and Otto didn't say that they loved each other, then they didn't love each other. Sal thought eventually that they *couldn't* name it. If it was love, then that had anxious implications of change; if it was simply friendship, then it had no justifiable basis for continuing as an affair. If it was neither, then there was no word for it and so it must be, necessarily, nothing.

'I don't know,' she said to Iris. 'There doesn't seem much point in going on with it.'

'Well, why not?' Iris said. 'You're fond of each other, it gives you pleasure – it's not hurting anyone.'

'Yes, I know.' But she thought it had the potential to hurt everyone, and what if that were for nothing important?

'Love is an act of will,' she said. One of Ariel's Catholic saints had said that, Ariel had quoted it to her when Sal insisted she didn't think she could ever become fond of the bluebottle Ariel brought her back from the beach as a pet.

'What *isn't*?' said Iris, and they laughed. Iris could always be relied on to see the relevance of offhand remarks.

And in lots of ways Sal had to admit the arrangement suited her. She could divide her week neatly – the one or two boozy nights with Otto and the other days to work or go out with her friends. Robert was still away. These were the weeks before she met Tony; she had persuaded herself that the power and the passion were not for her again. And later, when it was all over with Tony she would complain to Iris, too.

'Otto was so *good* about it.'

'Well?'

'Well, he could have at least been jealous, or showed that he was.'

51

'He probably didn't think he had the right to. It hasn't been that sort of relationship.'

'I don't know what sort it has been. That's the trouble.'

Robert was back in Sydney by then, and that was at least part of the trouble. Sal had had to go back to being a half-time parent and she hated that. And Robert was out of his conveniently labelled 'away' drawer. Nothing was clear any more. For some weeks she didn't see Otto at all, or only briefly, accidentally. She went to the coast for a fortnight and when she came back she had decided that the affair with Otto had dwindled away of its own accord. She was relieved.

Then in the wine bar one afternoon she saw him freshly and realised the attraction was still there, even if she could not put a name to it. She was piqued when he said he was working hard and that he'd call her the next week. And, she said to Iris later, she'd been celibate for weeks again; it wasn't healthy.

'No,' Iris agreed. 'Your skin starts to dry out.'

'That's the least of it . . .'

The worst of it was that with physical need came the memories of the days, years, with Robert, when they had filled every need in each other. Sal couldn't name the feeling she had for Robert now, either. It was love, certainly, she believed she would always love him, but it was also something more like a lack in herself, not quite as simple as loss, but a feeling of being without him. She didn't think she, or anyone else, would ever compensate for that. But she had thought she was used to it, had learned to accept that her life would always now contain that lack. Even being in love with Tony had not come near that space. She didn't want to think of Robert; she didn't want the old nights of futile *wanting* back again, not knowing what it was she wanted . . .

'Are you alright Sal? In yourself? You seem depressed.'

'Yeah, just drifting.' She made an effort. 'Spiro and

Leo say they're going to get their paisley suits whether you get married or not.'

They laughed. Iris's wedding was still being elaborated on, although no-one now had any real hope of it happening. Iris said they should have their dresses made too, just in case.

They were silent for a while, then Iris asked for the bill. At least, Sal thought, I know what I feel for my friends. Pure affection, the most uncomplicated love.

The women kissed in the street. 'Anyway,' Iris said, 'there's always Harry's lunch on Friday.'

'Yeah.' Sal laughed. 'I'll pin my hopes on that.'

She waited to see Iris hail a cab, then they waved and Sal ran across the road with the green light. She walked back along the wide, delapidated street, pleased that the crêpe myrtles were in full bloom. When she got home she emptied the vase of dying dahlias and cut fresh ginger flowers from the garden. Their honeysuckle scent surprised her when she walked through to the bathroom later, and, looking into the mirror, she thought she would ring Otto in the morning.

Acting

Rosemary Creswell

Sal had fallen in love again, with a visiting actor from the UK.

'Sal, why can't you fall in love with someone *easy*? Why do you always fall in love with these blow-ins from some other state or country? You'd fall in love with a bloody Martian if you knew he was pissing off the next day.'

That's what Leo said to her at the breakfast table in their large house after Sal had been going on about Paul for a bit. Sal said she wasn't in love and he wasn't, in any case, pissing off the next day. He was here for at least two weeks.

Her children were excited at the idea of a Martian.

Rosie was eight and said, 'Mummy, when can we meet the Martian, go on, when?' And Sarah who was fifteen said, 'Shut up stupid, there aren't any Martians in Sydney,' and glared at her mother and went on reading Georgette Heyer.

Iris, on the other hand, was much more sympathetic when Sal told her about Paul. Sal had met him at an interstate literary conference. He was a comedian, a satirist, and although she wasn't in love, she said, they had

54

nevertheless formed a very close friendship, a friendship she hoped would last, in fact was sure would last, and that was better, wouldn't you agree, than love?

Iris didn't believe her, about not being in love. She had heard Sal before talking about forming close friendships and not being in love, and she knew it really meant that she was in love and wanted to go to bed with this alleged close friend. Over the last year she had heard Sal say it about Otto and Tony and Alec. Now there was this Paul.

Sometimes, when challenged by Iris, Sal would say about these people, 'We–ell, I don't *think* I'm in love, I don't think I *love* him . . .'

Sal was saying this now about Paul, so Iris knew that Sal was in love.

They had, she told Iris, talked and dined and drunk together at the literary conference, but they hadn't made love, nor was she necessarily expecting or wanting to. Now that he had come to Sydney for a short season, she told Iris, she would see him and talk to him and continue this close friendship. They got on very well. They had much in common. His politics were sound. They laughed together a lot. He seemed to like her. She didn't care if they never went to bed. As a matter of fact, she told Iris, it would probably mess things up if they did. Only last night, she said, she had met him in the theatre-restaurant after the show and they had had drinks and supper till dawn and were just as close as ever and even though Jane, his publicity manager, was with them it didn't affect their close bond. And she had got to know Jane quite well, she told Iris, and liked her, because of the fact that Jane had been at every rendezvous they had had, including the ones at the interstate literary conference. Of course it was a bit of a bore in some ways, Jane always being there, but the closeness of Sal's friendship with Paul could withstand any impediment. And it wasn't as if Jane was some kind of watchdog, she was nice. There was, Sal told Iris, an almost mystical oneness that she shared with Paul so it didn't really matter if other people were around. And of course she *had* thought about going to bed with him but it was difficult and in any case it was probably preferable not to sully the spirituality of the friendship with anything carnal.

Was this Jane person *on* with him? Iris asked, and Sal said no.

A plan was forming in Iris's mind.

Sal told Iris all of this late one morning in Iris's office. Sal was looking tired because of having been up all night being close to Paul, but she said she was very happy. They had a lunchtime drink and then Sal had to go home. She had to go home suddenly when Louise from the wine bar looked at her and made a joke about would she like tripe and fried eggs for lunch. Besides, she was meeting Paul again tonight after the theatre and needed sleep.

Iris stayed on at the wine bar. She was thoughtful. She finished the small carafe of reisling and ordered another and drank it. She told Louise about her plan and Louise agreed it was a good one. At about three o'clock Iris went back to the office. She had definitely decided to help Sal out with the problem of this Jane person.

At four o'clock she rang her old friend John whom she hadn't seen for a year and asked him if he would like to have dinner with her. He was pleased. A long time ago they had been lovers but now they were just friends even though they sometimes went to bed. He arrived at the office in his Saab at about six and they had several glasses of wine in the office for old times sake and then a few scotches. They had pre-dinner drinks at the Riverview Hotel in Balmain.

After dinner in an expensive Balmain restaurant with Doric columns, an indoor fountain, statues, lashings of crystal, an elderly Viennese pianist and early twentieth century red wines, John suggested to Iris that she was a bit tired and perhaps they should go home.

Iris then explained.

'My great friend Sal is in love with a visiting actor,' she said, 'but can never get him on her own because his awful publicity manager, Jane, is forever hanging about. Could we go to the restaurant after his show, and I'll chat to Jane and divert her attention, we can talk about arts policy and publicity in Australia or something, and you pretend to flirt with Sal so that it appears she has hundreds of men in love with her so that he'll be jealous and will drag her away from you and take her to his hotel room?'

John saw his night with Iris retreating, but resigned himself to it and agreed. He was rich and intelligent and kind and handsome which was why Iris had picked him for the job.

'Alternatively,' suggested Iris, 'you could take this Jane character off to bed and I'll pretend to go to the toilet, but I'll really leave the restaurant, and leave Paul and Sal together. Or maybe after you've been with Jane for a while, you and I could meet up somewhere else and have a few drinks.'

John didn't seem quite so keen on the fallback plan, but he agreed anyway because he was fond of Iris and although he'd only met Sal twice any friend of Iris's was a friend of his and he would do his best to help out.

It was only ten o'clock and the curtain didn't fall until midnight, so they had to have some after dinner drinks at Arthur's nightclub to fill in the time.

When they arrived at the restaurant, Iris saw Sal sitting at a table with five people. She told John to wait at the bar. 'I'll be the forward scout,' she said, 'and assess the situation. When I give you the nod come over and greet us as if you've just arrived and be *very* affectionate to Sal.'

The people at the table were Paul, Sal and Jane and two arts journalists, from the *National Times*. Sal was pleased to see Iris and introduced her to her close friend Paul. She looked a lot better than she had at lunchtime. Paul was a bit distracted, what with doing interviews with the journalists, consulting with Jane, and talking to Sal. Iris could see that he was *very* good looking. She might have known it, Sal always went for good looking men even when she was saying she didn't care if they never went to bed.

Iris signalled to John. He arrived at the table and greeted Iris and Sal effusively. He met Paul. He met Jane. After a while the reporters finished with the interviewing and left. John positioned himself next to Sal. He was witty and charming and affectionate. He put his arm around Sal's shoulder, and she seemed puzzled and then annoyed, although Paul didn't notice any of this as he was busy consulting with Jane. John withdrew his attentions from Sal and looked to Iris for instructions. They were drinking martinis, or at least Iris was, she didn't know what the others were drinking. She indicated the alternative plan. John moved next to Jane and started to talk to her about the difficulties of promoting theatre in Australia while she listened politely with a who-the-fuck-are-you look on her face. Sal was looking more confused but went on talking to Paul. Iris was just drinking.

Paul decided to order some bottles of champagne to celebrate the evening. 'It's not every city in the world,' he said, 'where you meet a great woman like Sally,' and he put his arm around her.

Iris was not feeling well. She thought Paul was being sarcastic towards Sal and became angry. 'No, it's not,' she said, 'and you'd bloody well better be grateful.' Sal was wearing her silver follow-me-home-and-fuck-me shoes and used them to give Iris a kick under the table. But by now Iris knew that Sal didn't understand the way she was being exploited by this so-called actor from England, and it was now up to Iris to protect her from him.

John had abandoned all plans, and was gloomily drinking and occasionally trying to persuade Iris to come home with him. But she had a mission and she had to see it through. Paul still had his arm around Sal, and Iris even overheard his suggesting that they go for a picnic the next morning. Poor Sal, Iris knew it would be a disaster for her if she gave in to him. She leant across, knocking over a bottle of champagne, and reminded Sal that she was due to finish a short story for the new literary magazine in the *Australian* next week. As Sal's agent, it was Iris's responsibility to remind her of deadlines. Sal glared at her and ordered more champagne and sank back further into Paul's arms.

It was three o'clock and the whole strategy had to be changed. It was Iris's duty to sit Paul out, to take Sal home and explain to her how she was being used. It wasn't an easy task but it had to be done.

Eventually John went home to his wife.

Iris and Jane talked for a time, and it was true, she was nice. Paul and Sal talked intimately. What a rat, thought Iris, pretending to be nice to her when he's a roué and a philanderer. Never mind about his acting talent and his good looks. She decided to sober up by having a cleansing ale. She might, after all, have to sit here all night protecting Sal.

Other people seemed to come and go from the table, but Iris was scarcely aware of them except that they were all talking about what a great performance Paul had given. He was giving a great performance now too, Iris thought bitterly. They all seemed to like him. No doubt they were taken in by him too. She got to thinking about Phillip and how she loved him and how he had thought it best that they live separately. The more she thought about him the more she thought it was ridiculous that they should live apart. Just because he was writing a book and needed order and routine. A stupid idea, and she would tell him. Tonight.

Sal and Paul were laughing and holding hands.

At 4.30 the restaurant threw them out. Jane got a cab to go home. Paul and Sal walked towards his hotel, and Paul, putting a steadying hand on Iris's arm, asked her if she would like him to pay for a room at his hotel for the night. Of course not. He tried to call a cab for her, but she said she was alright thank you very much.

She had failed. She was miserable.

It was a short walk from Darlinghurst to Kings Cross where Phillip lived. She pressed the security buzzer for a long time and when he answered she said she had something to say to him. When he came to the door, sleep-creased and bleary, she was crying. She was crying for Sal who had been abducted and for all the Sals of this world. Phillip couldn't make any sense of what she was saying. She told him that she had come to talk out something important with him, but she wouldn't say what it was.

He undressed her and put her to bed.

At nine in the morning when she came to, she couldn't remember why she had been so unhappy but she was very excited and felt awful and so she put herself into a clinic for a few days rest. The doctor said she had been working too hard, overdoing things.

After she had been resting at the clinic for two days, a nurse gave her a message. Sal had phoned. The message said, 'Everything A-OK with Paul. Take care.' she rang Sal on the red phone but Sal was out with Paul. Leo answered and told her that things were going fine with Sal, that Paul was in love with her, that she was in love with him, that he was a good, nice man, and that later in the year Sal was thinking of moving to England to live.

Three Acts

Jean Bedford

Sal walked into the house and Leo looked up in surprise.

'Hello, darling. I didn't really expect you back today. I thought you'd probably elope with somebody in Perth.'

'Don't talk to me. I need a drink.' Sal was very shaky. She had drunk gallons of mineral water on the plane, now she wished she'd followed Ernest's example and had a few Scotches. He'd looked in much better shape at the airport.

'Well? Any festival fucks?'

'No,' Sal said, making her voice prim. 'Certainly not. I went there to work, and work I did.' She threw her case into the bedroom, then went in after it and got out the signed book of Sam Hunt's poetry that she'd brought back for Leo.

'Thanks.' He was pleased. 'Then this isn't a major hangover that I see before me?'

'It certainly is. Oh dear,' she poured herself a large glass of wine. 'In fact I nearly *didn't* come back today, but the organisers said I'd have to pay two hundred bucks to change my booking. I just managed to crawl down to the hotel lobby to say I was staying another day. But when they told me that – you've never seen anyone move so fast. I've left half my underwear at the hotel.'

'Well, tell me all about it. Did you have *fun*?'

She sat down and described the festival: the heat, the

61

crowded uncooled classrooms full of adolescents wondering who on earth these writers were, the famous international visitors, new Australian friends made quickly and now to be written to.

'Come on. There's more. What's that smirk about?'

'I never smirk,' said Sal, smirking. She got the festival brochure from her bag and flicked through it. 'I did meet probably the most gorgeous man on earth, though.' She handed Leo the brochure, 'See . . .'

'Right.' Leo's voice was deliberately weary as he looked at the photographs. 'So when's he coming to Sydney?'

'Shut up. It's not like that at all.' Sal took the leaflet from him and gazed at the pictures of Paul. 'I just happen to admire his work. He did a one-man show for the writers' session. He is really terrific.'

'And . . .?'

'And nothing. We had a few drinks together, lots of laughs. He's a lovely man, that's all.' She laughed. 'And he *is* coming to Sydney.'

'Sal!' Jenny's loud clear voice cut through the noise of the wine bar. 'Iris says you're in love *again*. Where do you get your energy?'

Sal got herself a glass and joined them. She was laughing, but she was irritated at this conspiracy of her friends.

'I am *not* in love, Jenny. And even if I were, it's at least six months in between.'

'An actor, isn't he?' Jenny was good at ignoring what other people said. 'That's no good. Actors are nightmares.'

Sal gave an exaggerated sigh. 'I am about to make an announcement: I have recently met an actor whose work I admire very much. He is a very nice man. I think we will be good friends. I hope to do some work with him. I am not, repeat not, in love.'

62

'No. They are. They're nightmares,' Jenny ploughed on and Sal glanced at Iris and smiled.

'Anyway,' Jenny said, 'have you slept with him?'

Sal gave up. 'Well . . . yes.'

'You can never trust them. They're always on stage.'

'Quite. Can we talk about something else now?'

Sal wasn't going to be drawn into the usual seductive analysis. If her friends were determined that she was in love, let *them* talk about it.

'Are you seeing him tonight?' Iris thought Sal was having a lend of herself.

'Oh, probably. I said I'd meet Leo after Paul's show, at the bar. I don't know – it's not like that.'

'What's he like?' Jenny could be very determined. 'Handsome, I suppose. You always go for handsome men. How many times have you fucked him?'

'Oh, for Christ's sake!' They were all laughing now. It was impossible to resist Jenny in this mood, which was her usual mood. Sal thought of all the generations of schoolchildren who must have found her incomprehensible – this respectable-looking middle-aged lady with her loud voice and foul tongue and eccentric habits.

'Do you want to know how often he goes to the bathroom, too?'

'Oh yes, why not?' Jenny laughed. 'Don't you want to talk about him?'

'I don't care one way or the other,' but they did change the subject.

Spiro was playing with his new Tarot pack, giving Sal a reading.

'There he is, Sal, in your outcome. And here's the travel card. It's a significant reading – there are no trivial cards here.'

'Hmm,' Sal said. 'That could equally well be Tony. And what about all this doubtful stuff?'

'I think they're about *your* doubts. Look at all the misery and confusion in the past cards. But the future's terrific.'

'I bet you say that to all the girls . . .'

'No. You can't get away from it. He's definitely there in your future.'

'Well, of course he is, I hope. Like all my friends.'

'All your friends aren't in this reading.'

'You're as bad as Iris.'

'And you're still clinging to *this*,' he pointed at the card that meant distrust, retreat, betrayal.

'Well, it's safer that way. Now let's do yours.'

A few weeks later Sal drove with the children to the coast for Easter, Chopin crashing from her car's tape deck as she wound between the high cliffs and the pounding sea. Leo was already at the house, with the fire lit. She unpacked her typewriter and the work she had brought with her and put them in her bedroom.

'There's wine in the fridge,' Leo said.

She poured herself a glass and stood by the big windows looking at the tide splashing in over the rock shelf. Everything relaxed, became clearer, down here.

'Has Paul gone?'

'Yes. At least as far as I'm concerned he has. I think he's probably going to stay the weekend in town, but for my purposes he's left – I've said *bon voyage*. Now I'd be quite happy if everyone'd forget all about it.'

'Ariel didn't like him.'

'She only met him for five minutes. Oh, I know – she distrusts men with that much charm. She thinks they'll break my heart.'

She made sandwiches for the jostling girls before they went to the beach. Then she set out her work on the desk and turned on the typewriter. She began to read what she had already written.

Sal was walking with the dog to the Lebanese milk bar to buy cat food. It was night-time and she hugged to herself the smell of frangipani and night-blooming jessamine from the gardens she passed. She walked jauntily, laughing at the silly dog twisting himself around in his pleasure to be out again that day. They had just come back from the coast and she had spent Easter working, working hard. She was pleased with herself and her life, the girls had had a good time, with their egg-hunt and its rhyming clues that she and Leo had made up, drunkenly, on Easter Saturday. Even Sarah, at fifteen, liked these childhood rituals.

Now she was thinking about Paul, who had gone back to London. She had been saving up thinking about him as a treat, a reward for working. Now she tried to focus on his charm, his sweetness and generosity, his fun. But she found herself coming back to his work, which she admired to the point of adoration. Like all actors, she thought, he was hard to get a fix on offstage – not that he was ever offstage, Jenny was right about that. Despite Iris and Leo and everyone else, she knew she hadn't been in love with him, but he had intrigued her deeply. It's been interesting, anyway, she thought, and that's the main thing. Oh, God, not to be bored. She glanced at the moon quickly, she was superstitious about such prayers.

'Excuse me.' It was a girl, about Sarah's age, with braces around her anxious smile. 'Do you know where the women's refuge is?'

'Yes, of course. No, hang on – is there one still here?' she called the dog sharply to her as she tried to think. 'Look, I *don't* know. But come up as far as the bookshop, they'll know.'

They did know and she asked the girl if she wanted to go to the milk bar with her while she bought cat food.

'Are you hungry? Have you eaten?' She waved vaguely

at the cabbage rolls and spinach omelettes in the glass counter.

'Yeah. I had chips at the station.'

'Where are you from?'

'Newcastle, I just got in on the train.'

On the way back to the refuge, which was less than a hundred yards from her own home, she asked the girl a bit about herself. She had been in and out of refuges and youth shelters since she was thirteen. Her father wouldn't have her at home – 'Not since the first time I got in trouble with the cops. Sorry, the police.'

'Have you been in trouble often?'

'Yeah. I dunno . . . I try to move to big places, places where it's hard to get in trouble – but, they seem to be watching you, you know?'

'Of course. They do watch you after the first time. That's how they operate.' She did know, too, had once done some research into girls 'exposed to moral danger' and their backgrounds. She felt she could have produced a case-history on the spot – cafés, dope, motor bikes, a brute of a father, probably incest, and a victimised, if not retarded mother. Then she was annoyed at herself for the stereotyped way she thought.

She knocked at an open lighted doorway and the dog bounded inside. A man came out from his television and showed them the right house. *Why* don't I know any more where the refuges are? she asked herself angrily.

Outside the fence she stopped. 'Look. Have you got any money?'

The girl turned out her pocket and held up a hand full of coins.

'Yeah. I got enough for food. But not for rent or anything, you know?'

'Here,' she fumbled in her purse, thanking heaven she'd cashed a cheque at the wine bar earlier, and gave her fifteen dollars.

'Jeez, thanks.'

'It's OK. I've got a daughter your age myself, and . . .' she trailed off. What could she say? What was she about to say? That she'd die a thousand deaths to see Sarah in this situation? Tactless bitch, she told herself savagely.

The woman at the refuge was cool, but helpful. They couldn't take her in, she'd have to go to a youth house, but she'd ring around for her. She looked at Sal curiously, who found herself talking for the girl, something she avoided with her own daughters. 'She's been in and out of shelters, apparently. I met her in the street.'

'Well, you were lucky, weren't you?' to the girl, who nodded. 'It's OK, we'll find her somewhere to sleep.'

Sal thrust into her bag again for some paper and wrote her name and phone number.

'Here. If you're ever . . . in trouble. Give me a ring.'

'Thanks. Thank you.'

Sal called the dog again and walked home, conscious of her good leather boots and the Italian cords she'd bought in London the last time she was there, the time of the holiday romance that had broken up her marriage. Even my fucking windcheater's a designer make, she thought.

She marched inside and plunked the milk and cat food down on the kitchen table. 'You'll just have to bloody wait,' she said to the bad-tempered tabby miaowing around her feet.

'What's the matter?' said Leo. 'Did you get my peanut bar?'

'Shit, no, I forgot. Listen,' and she told him about the girl. The children and Spiro came in as she talked and she had to repeat it.

'Why didn't you invite her here?' said Sarah. She would have liked a girl her own age in the house.

'Because . . .' she looked at Leo, then at Spiro.

'Because,' Spiro said, 'she's better off as she is. Those places are good now, they're not like prisons any more. The kids have autonomy, they're taught skills, they're fed, they get an allowance.'

'Yeah,' she said, 'but . . .'

'No, really,' Spiro said. 'They're a million times better off than with their families, and they've got a support group – zillions of times better off. I'd have preferred it to *my* family.'

Sal laughed. 'I know. I thought about all that. My first impulse of course was to bring her here. But what can you do?' She gestured at their comfortable living-room, the original paintings and cartoons on the walls, the sturdy children wide-eyed at this tragedy. 'Give her a look at all this, this lot with their dancing lessons and gymnastics and homework and everything else, and then dump her. Yeah, it all flashed through my head, don't worry.'

'We could have adopted her.' Things were simple to Rosie, at eight.

'No, darling, we couldn't. That's the point. Oh shit, come on, it's time you were in bed.'

She sat drinking white wine at the table with Leo. He was reading her outline, he seemed absorbed. She spoke away from him, to the dog, if anyone.

'You know, she didn't even have a bag? Just jeans and a V-necked pullover over her shirt. And a pocket full of small change. She didn't even have a bag.'

He didn't look up, but she thought he nodded. He spoke about her project and she got interested in that for a while. Then he said, suddenly, 'Don't worry about it. You did all you could.'

'Yeah. I know.' But the rest of her life seemed to have been trivialised, although she knew it was a temporary feeling. Trivial, the work she put so much of herself into, the healthy beautiful girls she adored, her planned trip to London, the man she had been keeping her thoughts for. She had intended to ring the refuge, to follow up, but now she thought she wouldn't. She would sound like a

busy do-gooder if she rang now, and she didn't know,
hadn't even asked, the girl's name.

Sal was at the coast again. She had been there all week,
by herself, she hadn't told any of her local friends she was
coming. She was spending the days working and recu-
perating from what seemed like an endless series of
debilitating emotions.

It was early evening; the sun had already gone down
behind the escarpment, but the day was still warm with a
false promise of spring. She was making a new garden by
the steps, with violets and ferns that would flourish under
the shade of the lemon-scented gum. When she heard the
phone ring she was tempted not to answer, then she
thought it might be something to do with one of the
children.

'Hello?' she was breathless from running up the steps.

'G'day.' It was Iris. 'I've just been to E.J.s.'

'Oh yes. Was it good?' One of Harry's lunches.

'Yeah. Tony was there, he asked after you.'

'Wow.' They both laughed, but Sal knew Iris could
sense her interest.

'I told him you were at the beach working, in case he
thought you hadn't been invited to lunch.'

'I wasn't.'

'I know. But . . .' She could imagine Iris's smile. She
smiled, too.

'Well . . .?' Sal knew Iris wouldn't ring just to say
she'd seen him.

'He said he's going to be back in Sydney next weekend. It was a message, Sal. There was no point in telling
me. He meant me to pass it on.'

'Like notes at school.' Sal hadn't thought of Tony at all
for months, she'd thought she'd forgotten him.

'He knows my phone number,' she said.

'Well,' Iris said, 'you know what they're like.'

'Sure do,' Sal said, but after she'd told Iris the work was going well and what a beautiful day it was down south, and hung up, she wondered. She went outside again and looked at the new cleared patch – the violets were already wilting in their puddles of water. She'd been peaceful, enclosed, now she felt restless and thought she'd walk on the beach.

Ploughing through the sand she remembered the time she'd brought Tony down here. They'd pulled dozens of starfish out of the rock pools and had a competition, arranging them according to colour, size, shape, speed and stupidity. The children were supposed to judge, but they'd been drawn in too. It had been a peaceful, bickering, laughing interlude in a time of surprising passion. She found herself wondering now if he would ring next weekend, and if he did, whether she would really want to see him.

'I'll just have to be out all weekend,' she said to Leo, at home. 'In case he doesn't ring.'

'What if he does?'

'I don't know. I wouldn't have thought I could be shaken by it still. But I am.'

It wasn't easy to be out every day and every night . . .

'Sal?'

'Yes, speaking. Tony? Are you in Sydney? How long for?'

'A few days. Are you free for dinner?'

'Sure. That'd be lovely.'

And then . . .

'You're quiet,' Tony said in the restaurant.

'Sorry, it probably wasn't a good idea to come.'

70

'Why not?' Wanting to know, apparently, at last wanting to know.

'Oh. It still hurts,' smiling, trying not to be too heavy. 'Even after all this time. Stupid, I know.'

'Not stupid. It still hurts me too.'

'Is that why you haven't . . . been in touch?'

'Yes. Of course. Didn't you know?'

'How long will it take, I wonder? Until we can be easy with each other?' Thinking, I'll never be easy with those bruised eyes, the dark slant of his jaw. 'Wanna make a date every six months to check?'

'No.' He wasn't always hesitant. 'Can we spend tonight together?'

'I don't know. What would it mean? I'd be upset either way, I think.' Trying to hold on to what she'd learned in the past months, what he'd taught her. Trying to be strong in her loneliness.

'Does it have to mean something?'

'Oh yes. It does.' Thinking, if this is the last time we see each other, at least I'll have been honest with him.

'Well, you know your Carroll. Things mean what we want them to mean.'

'No,' Sal said. 'That's *words*. Things don't, I find.'

But later, walking through the Cross, slightly drunk, relaxed with each other, she says 'Oh, why not? What's a fuck or two between friends anyway?'

And wakes up in the early hours terrified at the familiarity of his warm body beside hers, and dresses quickly, quietly and runs away home. And he rings at noon and says 'I missed you when I woke up.' And to her silence, 'Sal? Are you still there?'

'I don't know. Are you?'

'Yes, I think so. D'you want to talk about it?'

She thinks hard about all the times she has wanted to hear those words from him, has wanted some sign from him that there is still something between them that needs to be talked about.

'No,' she says. 'What's the use? Things haven't really changed, have they?' Once things have gone into this grinding gear, she thinks, you can never get it back to neutral.

'What are you laughing at?'

'Myself. Watcha doing?'

'Nothing much. Shall we do something?'

'No. I've got the children.' They are all at mates' places, or gym or acting class, but she doesn't want him there when they come home. She knows he is thinking that in the past the children made no difference, that they could have gone somewhere with them.

'Well . . .?'

She could suggest something to do this evening, she knows he is waiting for that, but she doesn't. Her mind is full of the things she could be telling him, how hurt and alone she has been, how they can't start from scratch, that she can't recover the insouciance she might have had before, how this time she would be watchful, demanding, would want it on her terms.

So she says to him, 'It wouldn't work. You were probably right the first time.'

'Are you sure, Sal?'

And she is surprised at how little pleasure she gets from the sense of him wanting her.

'Yeah. I'll send you a postcard from London.' He knows she is not going for another three months, if at all.

'OK.' And, after one of his silences, 'Thanks for last night, anyway. It was terrific.'

It always was terrific, she thinks when she has put the phone down and crawled back to bed for what Iris calls her narcosis therapy. Silly fucker, why'd it take him so long to find out?

Or . . .

'Sal?'

'Tony? Are you here? How long for?'

'Till tomorrow. Are you free for dinner?'

'Well . . . yes. No, I don't think so.'

'Oh.' God, how she remembered their silences on the telephone.

'I know how you hate to talk about things. And if I saw you just now I'd want to talk. Deeply and meaningfully.' She laughed, 'Not a very good idea, probably.'

'I don't know.' She could sense an unusual willingness in him to talk.

'Well, I do,' she paused. 'I've become quite good at the verbal reticence, too.'

'I'd like to talk,' he said.

'No,' she was definite. 'There's no point.'

'Are you sure?'

'Yep, it's too late for all that.' And she could be proud as she hung up at how far she had progressed in a few months, how tough she could be in her loneliness . . .

But in fact she was out enough over the weekend not to be there if he had called, and as far as she knew he hadn't. But she was shaken for a week or so over the possibilities, imagining the phone calls, her being strong, or weak. The potential reconciliation, the potential and final separation.

So that when he did appear, unexpectedly, a week or two later, for a few days, and they spent most of their time together, falling into bed as naturally as if there had not been the months of estrangement, with no deep-and-meaningfuls, no statements, taking up almost, almost, as if what had happened before had not happened, she was surprised at how little fuss there was, after all.

Alma Mater

Rosemary Creswell

It wasn't until Iris was in her third year of university that she had started to make proper friends. Probably this was because she hadn't gone full-time until then, and at evening classes you didn't have much time to do anything. In her third year she had made friends with Jill and with Karen.

Jill was a very tall thin girl. She had small brown freckles spattered all over her lovely slender face, the kind of freckles that when Iris had them as a child she used to spend hours every day rubbing oatmeal and lemon all over her face to bleach them off. And Jill's two front teeth crossed over each other slightly which made her look shy like a rabbit. Her fine brown hair was fringed across her pale eyes and her soft voice had a perpetual shake in it which made her seem even more fragile and tentative than her thin body suggested. Her bones stuck out at her hips, pushing at the bleached denim they all wore then, and she rolled her own with delicate nail-chewed fingers.

Jill was a feminist before anyone else in that year. Her quiet jittering voice pushed through the microphone at front lawn moratorium meetings, accusing the male demonstrators of being sexist warmongering pigs. She said the war was in the kitchen not in Vietnam. Her coarse language trembled warnings at them. She clenched her angular fist and waved her skinny arm in the air and proclaimed sisterhood. She wrote fine poems which were a mixture of romantic wailing country and western songs, stern threatening feminist lines and lyrics of loneliness.

She decided she was a lesbian. She fell in love with Gertrude Stein and Virginia Wolfe and Djuna Barnes. She talked about how men killed Sylvia Plath.

Sometimes she didn't get out of bed for a week on end, and Iris and Karen were summoned to her patchwork-quilted bedside and asked to go out and buy her flagons of riesling and packets of Drum. Her room was very dark, in a basement flat in Glebe. She had a diminutive female Siamese cat which, when it wasn't hanging like a bat off the dark patterned brocade curtains, skittered across the bed and around the room, as speedy and nervous as Jill herself.

Jill went to the pub one night with Karen and they stayed till closing time. Then they went back to Karen's for more wine and they went to bed with each other and made love. The next day in the coffee shop at the university, Jill, shaking more than usual because of her hangover, told everyone she was in love with Karen. It was the first time for both of them.

The trouble was that quite soon Jill began to despise Karen, but Karen was in love with Jill.

Karen was a pretty and softly spoken fair-haired girl who laughed a lot of the time. She would smile and her smile trusted everyone, even the people who did awful things to her, like boyfriends who didn't take her out but climbed in her bedroom window drunk at two a.m. on their way home from parties to fuck her. She would always lend money to people, from her scholarship allowance, and give them lifts in her battered old car, and buy round after round of beer in the pub for anyone who asked. She fell in love with Jill but Jill was awful to her and soon began to speak about her in the deriding triumphant tone that men sometimes use when they fuck women once and then ignore them.

Iris was older than most of her university friends, because she had gone there late. She was living with Matthew whom she loved and who was fifteen years older than her and who was called a captain of industry by her male university friends because he worked in business. He liked her younger female university friends and would often drink with them in the university pub in the evenings and on the weekends. He had once been a clinical psychologist and he would talk to them in a wise fatherly way about their problems. He would tell them about his own university days when you had to bring your own candles to night-time lectures because of the post-war electricity blackouts, and about how most of the students were Commonwealth Reconstruction Students out of the army now the war was finished. All the most neurotic girls in Iris's year fell in love with him and he counselled the best looking ones in the pub after work. When Iris first met him he was living with his wife, but after five years he moved out to live with Iris in a narrow single story terrace in Forest Lodge near the university.

At the end of third year Iris held a party during the afternoon to celebrate the end of the exams. Forty people came and they ate and drank and some smoked dope in the tiny back garden. Matthew came home from work late at eight o'clock. He stood among the flattened paper cups and bladders torn from wine casks to squeeze out the last drops. Joni Mitchell sang of dark clouds and being a country station and a wild flower. He drank a few beers for sociability and then went to bed.

The party went on and on. Some people were sick. Some stayed inside and played records and danced. A poet went to sleep on the kitchen floor. A different poet's wife fell into the bathtub of melting ice for the beer and stayed there for the cool. A decorous English lecturer left the party in his wine-soaked Italian linen suit, barefooted, escorting a first year student with one suntanned breast falling out of her sundress. Jill lay on the grass and cried and cried and cried and said she wanted to kill herself. She talked about Sylvia Plath and Marilyn Monroe and Virginia Wolfe. After a while someone picked up her crumpled angular body and took her home to her smothering basement.

In the end, in the garden, were just Iris and Karen and David, also from their year. They sat on the steps outside the kitchen drinking the wine dregs from the silver bladders held high over their mouths like Spanish gourds. While David talked about Anthony Powell and the music of time, Karen began to stroke Iris's neck, gently massaging it and then putting her hands down Iris's shirt and touching her nipples. She kissed the back of Iris's neck, softly, her warm breath in the warm night.

David was embarrassed and climbed over the fence and left.

Karen whispered to Iris that she loved her, and they kissed with their tongues and touched each other's faces, reverently, as though they had not really seen each other before, as though the night had reshaped them. The dark red bougainvillea arched over them and its thorned branches wove into the passionfruit vine twisting around the palings. Iris's tortoiseshell cat sat on the steps and yellowed its eyes at them. Then they lay full out on the grass and Karen kissed Iris all the way down her chest and on her belly.

From inside Dory Previn yelled about doing it alone in a forty mile zone, to the empty house except for Matthew and the lights shining on.

Karen and Iris were intertwined. They went into the study at the front of the house and stood and kissed each other with their shirts off, trailing their hands down each other's backs.

Iris didn't know what to do next. She wanted Karen to

keep touching her and she wanted to keep touching Karen. But she was too frightened to get into the bed in the study. It was too difficult. Too complicated. Too far away from the way she saw herself.

So she said, 'Let's get into bed with Matthew.' She did not know why she said this. It seemed as if it would create mitigating circumstances for what they were doing. It would ameloriate things, somehow legitimise them, or take the burden of guilt off her. As though, somehow, Matthew had started it all. It would appear more accidental, or more normal.

So they undressed in the study and went into the bedroom and climbed into the large bed across which Matthew was lying diagonally, the sheets pushed off in the hot night, and lightly snoring. Iris climbed in on one side of him and Karen climbed in on the other, and they began to caress each other across his back. He stirred, slightly irritated in his sleep. Bloody Iris getting into bed and breaking his sleep. He shifted about, punching into the pillow. Then he woke up, suddenly, feeling around him. There were more than two arms and two legs and two breasts. He didn't care whose they were. Matthew: forty-five, with Iris thirty and Karen twenty-one, all naked in the one bed. For years later he would talk about it to some of his office colleagues at after-work drinks. He kissed both their breasts. He took turns to put his hand inside both their thighs and touch their cunts. He fucked Iris while she kissed Karen. Iris felt more comfortable about things.

At four in the morning the phone rang. Matthew climbed out of bed. He strode across the room to answer it. He wished phones were televised things so that whoever was on the other end of it could see what he was doing.

It was North Ryde Hospital.

Iris took the phone from Matthew. The sister was curtly saying that Jill was there. That she had swallowed a lot of valium but was perfectly alright. She said it in a tone which suggested that everyone knew you couldn't die from valium and it was all inconvenient not to mention inconsiderate.

The phone call shocked them. It made what they had been doing seem thoughtless, even, perhaps, the cause of Jill's overdose.

They covered themselves up and in the morning Matthew drove them to the hospital, Iris and Karen holding flowers and flasks of Chateau Tanunda for Jill which Matthew said was irresponsible in the light of what was already in her system. She's got the smallest stomach in the world, he said, and it's already full of diazepam.

In the car they sat carefully separated in the front seat, making sure no part of their skin or clothing touched each other's.

Jill was in a light airy ward, its white nylon curtains shifting in the tepid breeze. The walls were shiny cream and the bedspreads that open-weave cotton that looks like your grandmother crocheted it. They found her behind a fabric screen, her freckled face paler than ever reposed on the snowy pillow, eyes closed and the Drum-stained chewed fingers curled on the bedspread and sporadically twitching. She was like some delicate insect that had been pulled out of a cave by an entomologist and placed there, in the light, to see what would happen.

Iris and Karen and Matthew felt gross. What they did in the night was accused by Jill's thin stillness. Their hands seemed enormous insensitive things.

Karen bent down and kissed Jill on the cheek. She shifted and then opened her eyes. 'You needn't have come here,' she said, 'I only did it to get away from you all for a while.' And she closed her eyes and rolled away from them.

Karen put the flowers in vases and wrapped up the

flasks in the florist's paper and put them in the bottom drawer of Jill's cupboard, on top of Jill's tiny pants and folded up jeans. She pulled a page out of her diary and wrote, 'We all love you, lots and lots,' and signed it *Karen*. And Iris wrote *Love, Iris* and Matthew wrote *Keep Your Chin Up, Matthew*, with a cross for a kiss.

Then they left and went to the pub for the whole day.

In the weeks afterwards Matthew tried to make it all happen again, but neither Karen nor Iris had the heart for it. Jill came out of hospital and stopped drinking and wrote more poems.

In the months afterwards, Karen and Iris went to bed together a few times and it was good but not really Iris's 'scene', as she said apologetically to Karen. And once, when Iris went to the laundromat one Saturday morning and came home to find Karen and Matthew sunbaking in the back garden, she knew they had been fucking. But she didn't mind. It sort of seemed the natural way to conclude the episode.

In the years afterwards, Karen and Jill and Iris finished their university degrees. Karen had long affairs, sometimes steady and loving, sometimes stormy and painful, with women. Matthew left Iris to live with a woman in another city, but after some dreadful vitriolic exchanges they became friends again. Jill went to New York to be alone and write poetry. And Iris stayed in Sydney, sometimes alone, sometimes having long neurotic sequences of casual fucks with men, sometimes having pleasurable affairs with men, and eventually falling in love with Phillip. Karen and Iris now lived in different Australian cities and still loved each other.

Iris told all this to Sal one night when they were talking about lesbianism and whether it was for them or not.

Watching
Jean Bedford

Sal had met Paul in Perth. She was with Freda, an inter-state writer whom Sal had not met before, but whose books she admired. The women had become immediate friends and were enjoying doing the conference together. Freda was older than Sal but she still fell in and out of love and laughed about it, and it was Freda who really fell in love with Paul.

They both came out into the coffee-room after his performance, and saw him by the counter.

'I'm going to tell him how terrific it was,' Sal said. 'You know what it's like when you've read and no-one comes up to you.'

'Yes! Tell him to have coffee with us. Tell him I adore him,' said Freda, her pretty face screwed into a lovesick expression.

He seemed pleased to be invited to join them and delighted, if a bit nonplussed, at Freda's declarations of eternal slavery and her offers to get down on the linoleum to kiss his feet. Freda had a copy of one of her books with her and she signed it and gave it to him, not letting Sal see what she had written. Sal thought two could play at that and went to the stall to buy one of her own books to give him, but he insisted on paying for it. She wrote 'Whatever Freda said, with knobs on.' He sat with them for a while and laughed a lot. When he left they arranged to meet again for a drink and Freda languished over him all the way back to the hotel.

'You have him, Sal' she said. 'You're younger than I am. I don't think I could survive it.'

On the night they were to meet him Freda insisted on staying in her hotel room. She would, she said, meditate and calm herself and pray to have Paul in her next incarnation. 'Though the way the gods work,' she said, 'he'll probably be my father or the local leper or something.'

Sal met him for a drink which turned into hundreds of drinks because he had just heard he'd been booked to go to Sydney and he wanted to see Sydney very much so he bought French champagne for hours and lots of people came and went and Sal staggered back to the hotel very late and couldn't remember much the next morning, which made Freda distinctly irritated with her.

'You'd better lift your game in Sydney,' Freda said. 'You're doing this for both of us, you know.'

'I've given him my phone number,' Sal said. 'What more can I do?'

'You could have dragged him bodily back to your hotel room.'

Sal laughed, 'I think there was a bit of a queue for that.'

Freda said, 'Well, he'd better ring you in Sydney.'

But in Sydney when they met it was by accident. Sal was having dinner with Ariel and she had just seen the notices of Paul's forthcoming show in the foyer of the theatre-restaurant.

'That's him,' she said to Ariel. 'That's the fantastic actor I told you about. You must come and see him.'

She and Ariel were both feeling at a loose end. Ariel's marriage had broken up a few months before and she was finding it more difficult to get over than she had thought. Sal kept telling her it would take at least eighteen months

for the grief and loneliness to ease – she meant this to
buoy Ariel up, to show that she was not morbidly unusual, but it had only depressed her further. So over
dinner they had decided that they would both go to England for a holiday later in the year and rage around
London for a couple of months. 'A change of scene,' Sal
said. 'That's what we both need. An adventure.'

They were drinking to that – Sal in champagne and
Ariel in mineral water with a twist of lemon, when Sal
saw Paul walk past the window, coming into the restaurant. She stood up, spilling her drink, and waved to
him. He was in a suit, with a few people in dinner dress;
they had clearly been to the opera or to some fancy
theatre.

'Sal!' He hugged her and turned to the people he was
with. 'This is her! This is the Sal I was saying I must
ring.'

'Well, why haven't you?' she said. She knew two of his
companions – one was the publicist for the theatre and
the other was a journalist she had once worked with.
Neither seemed particularly overjoyed that Paul had
found her. Sal didn't care, she took his arm and led him
over to meet Ariel, who also didn't seem overjoyed.

'I've got to have dinner with some people,' he said.
'But, Sal, come and join us, will you?' He moved away,
his hands held out from his body in a shrug.

'He's very good looking,' Ariel said. 'If you like dark
men with melting brown eyes.'

Ariel only liked men who were blond and blue-eyed,
because at the age of twelve she had been passionately in
love with a nordic thirteen-year old and, she claimed, his
image was indelibly patterned onto her love-synapses.

'He's not, really,' Sal said. 'His face is just very mobile
and alive.' She couldn't help the excitement in her voice.
She wanted Ariel to like him too.

'Well, I've got to go. You go and drink champagne
with him, my dear. Have a good time.'

They kissed and Sal joined Paul at his table, where there were other people she knew, too, and they drank champagne and held hands and exclaimed over each other. His agent for this tour seemed a bit put out at Sal's presence, and Sal thought she had probably fallen in love with him already. He was the sort of man that women fell in love with, he invited it, with his friendly flirtatious charm and his genuine interest in other people. He whispered to Sal, 'Do you know *everybody* in Sydney?'

'Sure,' she said. 'Stick with me, kid.'

But Jane, his Australian agent, had obviously decided to stick with Sal too, and when it turned out they both lived in the same suburb it was impossible not to agree to share the taxi, dropping Paul at his hotel. He invited them in because he said he wanted to talk to Sal about one of the shows he was doing, to get her opinion of how it would go down in Sydney, and perhaps to get some local references that would fit. She was very flattered to be asked but said she was a little too gone on champagne to make sensible comments.

'Never mind,' Paul said. 'Come in for a nightcap anyway.'

The nightcap turned into a drinking and talking session in the foyer of the Southern Cross that lasted until four a.m. The journalist from the restaurant turned up, too, with his girlfriend, looking for late night drinks, and Sal noted how Paul had already charmed the hotel staff into being perfectly amiable about keeping the bar open this long.

Before she left they arranged to meet the next day for lunch and to go over Paul's script. In the final taxi home Jane quizzed Sal about how well she knew Paul and seemed satisfied to hear it was a recent and fairly casual acquaintance. Sal wondered if Paul had this effect on women wherever he went and thought it must be very tiring to have people fall in love with you all the time. Still, he seemed to have lots of energy.

'*We're* the monsters,' she said to him after they had been through his script. She had sat entranced while he performed at what he said was low intensity, completely drawn in, forgetting that she was supposed to be listening for a purpose, but rallying enough afterwards to make a few suggestions and give him a couple of local jokes. The piece had talked about monsters, about those who watched life without being part of it, Shakespeare's 'They' who have the power to hurt and will do none, the lilies that when they fester smell far worse than weeds. Now they were at the Malaya, eating. Sal was still shaken by his performance and his insights.

'What do you mean?'

'Well, we not only watch life and what other people do and then make . . . artefacts out of it, we also watch ourselves watching. We watch others watching us watching . . . We have no real core, people like us, no part of us that isn't, somehow, able to be detached and made self-conscious.'

'Shifting sands?' he said.

'Well, yes. I mean, we do live, we are affected by life. When we are pricked do we not bleed, etc. We are hurt by other people, we love genuinely, all that, but we never stop watching and we always know we will be able, sometime, to *use* it.'

'Preying animals. Do you think we are?'

'No, not quite. I don't think we deliberately do things, make choices, so as to use them, but we always know we can. We've got an escape route from the . . . I don't know, the awful finality of life or something.'

'And that makes us monsters? Doesn't it also mean that some of us have a heightened sense of responsibility, too? That we can watch on behalf of those who don't?'

'Yes, perhaps.' She laughed, 'Yeah. We're saints, not monsters.'

They ordered another bottle of wine and Sal told him the new batch of New Zealand jokes, and he told her the Irish jokes from London. He had to go back to the hotel for a newspaper interview and insisted Sal come too. She let herself be carried along by him, she knew that feeling of wanting to go with whatever was happening at the time, not wanting interruptions to spells of uncomplicated pleasure. She thought if they lived in the same city they would be bad for each other as friends, always egging each other on to excitement, neither willing to ever stop the good times rolling.

She said something of this in the taxi. He was pleased at the idea. 'Well, when you come to London we can test it. Non-stop entertainment for weeks on end. But, I think you're really not like that all the time. I think, like me, you probably go on binges and then lock yourself away to work. You must, or you'd never get your books written.'

'I often wonder how I do. I think the elves come in while I'm asleep and do it for me.'

'Like Lowry's invisible workmen monkeying with it during the night . . .'

'Yeah. Me and Malcolm Lowry.'

They laughed and looked at each other with appreciation.

Jane was waiting for him in the foyer and seemed annoyed to see Sal get out of the taxi too and link her arm in his.

'I won't interrupt the interview,' Sal said. 'I'll just sit quietly in a corner and drink.'

Jane accepted the inevitable. 'Well, I'll sit with you, and we needn't be that quiet.' While they waited for Paul they talked. Sal and Jane had known each other casually and professionally for a few years, but they had never talked to each other much. Now Sal decided she liked

Jane and hoped Jane liked her too.

'I should go,' she said to Paul, when he and his interviewer joined them.

'No,' Jane said. 'We were just going out to dinner at Bondi to show Paul the sea. Why don't you come too?'

Sal was surprised at the generosity in this, Jane would have clearly preferred to have Paul to herself.

'Well, I might,' she said, 'but I'll have to go home first and change and feed the cats. Give me a ring when you're about to go.' She thought she'd leave it up to Paul – if he rang she would go, but she didn't want to join the ranks of his adoring fans.

He did ring and she joined them and they went to Bondi and ended up sitting on the beach all night to watch the sun rise. Some other friends of Paul's were there, too, people he had known in London, but most of them drifted away until only Sal and Jane and Paul were left.

'Come for a walk to the end of the beach,' Paul said. 'We need exercise.'

'OK,' said Sal, but Jane had gone very quiet and she said she would wait on the steps for them.

'Is Jane alright?' she said, when they had raced each other to the wading pool and collapsed breathless on the rocks.

'I think Bondi has bad associations for her,' Paul said. 'Something to do with her husband and the babies that were killed.'

'What? I didn't even know she'd been married. Jesus – *babies*? Plural? I've been ranting on to her all day about my gorgeous girls and how lovely it is to be a mother. Shit.'

'Yes. She was telling me about it the other night. Twins. A car accident, a long time ago, but it's near the anniversary I think.'

Sal was silent. She thought Paul must also be the recipient of lots of confidences from people.

'You're a very kind man, aren't you?' She said. 'You should be careful. It can exhaust you, being kind to everyone.' She wondered if she included herself.

'Come on,' she said. 'Let's get back to Jane.'

Jane was sitting on the steps with tears running down her face and Sal sat beside her and put her arm around her shoulder.

'I shouldn't have come here,' Jane said. 'I'll have to go home.'

Sal offered to go with her but Jane said she wanted to be by herself so they hailed a cab and then Sal and Paul decided to have breakfast in a pancake café. They stared at each other with wide sleepless eyes.

'Thank God I'm going away for the weekend,' she said. 'I don't think I can stand the pace.' Everything seemed sharpened by her tiredness, she could see almost through the fine dry skin on her hands to the veins and bones beneath. Paul, unshaven and untidy, looked much younger and Sal had a pang of remembering Robert on the days he didn't shave and lounged around in his old shorts and thought that it was one of the things she missed about being married.

Paul looked disappointed. 'Are you? Where are you going?'

'To the mountains. You should get someone to take you for a drive around there, it's very beautiful.' She thought of offering, inviting him up for the day, but, again, she didn't want to be considered simply among those who were eager for his company. She also felt, already, that she knew him well enough to know that his disappointment, though real at the time, would not last. It was partly why he was such a superlative actor – he felt what he did at any time, genuinely meant what he said, but he was capable of doing and saying many different things with many different people. She understood that. 'We're anybody's' he had said to her in the Malaya, and she had known exactly what he meant.

Sal and Leo drove to the mountains that afternoon, after Sal had had a little sleep. They were going to Phillip's shack and were both looking forward to a few days out of Sydney. Leo was having problems with his love life and wanted to be incommunicado, Sal was on edge now about Paul and thought it was a good idea to get away and think about it.

'The trouble is,' she said to Leo, over the tape of Scottish and Irish folk songs that they always played on long drives together, 'that I do lust after his body. But we seem to be becoming such close friends that I don't want to spoil it. You know how sex always fucks everything up.'

'Well he's only here for a few weeks. What's it matter?' Leo went back to his tuneless and lusty accompaniment of 'Bonnie Doon' and Sal drove on in silence.

'It's quiet in the country, isn't it?' Leo said doubtfully when they reached the shack. It was on the edge of the bluegum forest and its yard ran down to a tangled gully of ferns and blackberries and small trees. They both took deep breaths of the cold mountain air, then investigated the living arrangements. The dog ran around barking madly at the unfamiliar scents outside and Leo got in an armful of wood. Sal put on a leg of lamb to roast and started peeling potatoes.

'I feel like Bert Facey,' Leo said later as they sat by the fire with glasses of claret, reading, the dog curled up at their feet. Leo had baggsed the rocking chair and its regular motion made Sal very drowsy.

'You look like him, too,' she said, 'you dag. Though he'd probably be getting up to make a cup of tea about now. I'd like mine in bed.'

In the night she woke up from a nightmare, still crying

out. She had had a falling dream, had been about to die, suddenly and painfully, in terror. She listened to see if it had woken Leo, but there was no sound from his room. When she told him about it in the morning he said it meant she was afraid of falling from a great height and dying.

'Thanks, Dr Jung. Why don't you and the good dog go and buy the newspaper and I'll cook breakfast.'

'Jesus,' Leo said, coming back with the papers. 'I can see what you mean.' He held up a page interview with Paul that had a large photograph of him smiling intensely into the camera. 'What a hunk.'

'What a *poseur*,' Sal said, smiling at the picture. 'That's his "I'm just a gorgeous little boy who'd love to be loved" look.'

'You're mentioned, honey.'

'Where? Let me see.' She read the piece and the line that said that a Sydney writer had given him invaluable help with his 'Monsters' script. 'Well,' she said, delighted, 'isn't that nice of him?'

'Give him a ring.'

'No – I'm still inclined to the we-are-just-good-friends attitude.' But she thought about him for the rest of the weekend while she pottered around and Leo worked on his thesis about Alexander Pope, and she wondered how much she did want to have an affair with Paul and how honest she was being with herself about their friendship. Leo had propped his picture against the sideboard, beside Phillip's copy of *War And Peace*, and they both mimed adoration at it whenever they passed.

'I wonder how much is just wanting the feeling of being in love again,' she said on the drive home. 'Just a relief from boredom?'

'All of it,' Leo said. 'Otherwise people'd never fall in love.'

'So young and so cynical,' Sal said. 'You read too much Pope.'

She rang Paul that evening and he said he'd missed her. She thanked him for the mention in the paper and he apologised for the wimpy photograph – 'I think I was thinking about a drink, at the time,' he said.

'Speaking of which . . .'

'Love to. Actually there's a dinner at Jane's tonight. She said to invite you if I saw you.'

It was hard to know what he thought, Sal realised as she put the phone down. He clearly wanted to see her, but was it because her company was a relief, that he could relax with her because they had such easy rapport and there was no threat of anything more than friendship? She tried to imagine what it would be like to be someone that other people were always falling in love with and decided that it *would* be a relief. 'Still,' she said to Leo, 'I can fuck him without falling in love with him, can't I?'

'Oh yeah?'

She laughed, 'Sure I can.'

'I knew this would happen,' she said to Paul. They were sitting in an all-night coffee-lounge in the Cross in the early hours of the morning.

'Did you? It was *all* news to me.' He was teasing her, trying to regain the space that had been between them, despite their mutual intensity. 'What is it? Admitting impediments?'

She laughed, 'To the marriage of true minds? Absolutely. And that was all about what a lie it all is, too.'

He declaimed the whole sonnet, *sotto voce*, with his trained Shakespearian rhythms and she joined in with the last lines –

'If this be error, and upon me proved,
I never writ, nor no man ever lov'd.'

'Sal,' he said, 'I know what you mean. That once sexu-

ality has entered – excuse the expression – then friendships change. But it doesn't have to be like that, does it?
Can't we trust each other as friends, anyway?'

'Perhaps *you* can,' she said. 'You're . . . freer than I
am. You're a bloke.'

He laughed so loudly that people turned around to
watch. 'I love you, Sal. You're quite mad. But seriously,'
he made his face very earnest and his voice took on the
intonation of an in-depth television interviewer. 'But
seriously. If it's making you uncomfortable then perhaps
we shouldn't go on with it. Let's just call it an aberration
and forget it.'

'It might be best.' They talked on, Sal relaxing in their
easy intimacy, about sexuality and what it does to people
and how it wrecked friendships and caused anxiety and
watchfulness and lack of trust, and then they got up to
go.

'Well,' Paul said, 'I suppose a fuck'd be out of the
question?' He'd become enamoured of this particularly
Australian expression.

'*You're* the mad one.' She took his arm and, laughing,
they hailed a taxi and went for the second time back to his
hotel room.

The first time had been after Jane's dinner, after hours
of talking and singing and dancing, when Sal had finally
said 'Your place or mine?' and he had turned his laughing
face to her and said 'Really?'

And in bed it had been delightful, eager and affectionate, talking and laughing and fucking all mixed up.
But in the morning she had felt tense and strained, and
they had breakfasted on the hotel's roof-deck and winced
at the bright sunlight reflected off the blue pool, and,
knowing that he trusted her to do so, she had carefully,
one by one, discounted all the words of passion and need
and love that had been spoken during the night.

The Monstrous Regiment

Rosemary Creswell

Iris and Sal were discussing dissension in the women's movement. They talked about the futility of sisters fighting with each other. About how they should unite to defeat the Enemy.

'Women,' said Sal, 'should never fall out among themselves over a man. Wives should become friends with mistresses. Even better, lovers with mistresses – to subvert the husband.'

Iris agreed entirely. 'And girlfriends should become girlfriends with the mistress as well.'

'There is the odd exception, though,' Sal said. 'Like Bronwyn.'

Bronwyn was an ex-girlfriend of Sal's ex-husband. To the best of Sal's knowledge, Sal's ex-husband hadn't seen this ex-girlfriend for many years, but she loomed threateningly large in Sal's mind whenever she had nothing else to think about. She called her 'the boring Bronwyn' and maintained it would be impossible to unite with her on anything, let alone ever become her lover. ('Ugh, yuk, imagine,' said Sal, who had never had an affair with a woman.)

Basically, whenever she had nothing else to think about, Sal hoped that Bronwyn would soon die a slow and painful death.

'How could he have been on with her?' she would ask.

If you didn't know the history of Sal's marriage you would think that Bronwyn was still with Sal's ex-husband. You would think that he had left Sal for Bronwyn, when it was all about eight years ago, and had only lasted two months anyway. You could tell Sal was in between love affairs when she started thinking about Bronwyn.

One of the ways she wanted her ex-husband to be punished was for him to have another affair with Bronwyn. She thought she was that awful. She hoped they would fall in love again and have a terrible life together. She hoped that in this new love affair they would have, there would be vicious fights, lots of misery, economic hardship, and either infertility or unwanted pregnancies, but that they would somehow be stuck together for life.

But apart from Bronwyn, Sal agreed that women should become friends and unite against the man.

Iris agreed entirely with this principle of the odd exception. She would listen to Sal going on about Bronwyn and agree. She even added more nasty details to the hideous life that Sal's ex-husband and Bronwyn would have if only they would get back together, to the point where even Sal thought it was a bit off – though she was grateful for the support.

A few years ago Iris herself had experienced an odd exception to the unity of women. At the time she had been having a pleasant affair with her old friend Pete. Before that she hadn't seen him for a year or two, except distantly at a crowded nightclub or cocktail bar when he was usually noisily holding forth on something or other or laughing very loudly. So when they more or less accidentally got together in a sexual way, all their friends thought it was a good idea and wished them well because they had both been unattached for quite a while and Sydney likes to see its denizens getting together, even if it's only for a night or two.

95

They had been together like this (less than lovers, more than friends, was how their friend Corrie described it) for about eight months when Pete, driving her home from dinner one night, told her that his friend Barbara from New York was arriving the next day to stay with him 'for about a month or so'. Iris didn't know who Barbara was and coming from an old libertarian school and not wanting to appear to care, didn't ask. And Pete, also from an old libertarian school and also being too awkward to explain things, didn't tell her.

After about a week of going about visibly not caring, and carefully avoiding going to any parties or places where she might see them together, she sent a typed message to his office by express courier. It said, 'Hope you are having fun. Don't expect to be served by any restaurants in Sydney – although you still might be able to get into *The Black Stump* or the cafetaria in the Zoo where unfortunately I don't have any clout, but they're the kind of places that would be about her style I imagine. Love, Iris.' She had calculated that the tone of this was about right, humorous but aggressive, a bit flippant and still not caring. It would elicit, she felt, some kind of response.

Another week went by and she still hadn't heard anything from or about him and Barbara. She was still assiduously not minding about it, despite comments from Sal and Peg and Jenny and Di that he was being an arsehole and she shouldn't take it lying down. (They weren't from the old libertarian school and didn't understand these things.)

After a month, a dozen or so of her women friends rang to say that they had been seen together at the gala opening of the Sydney Film Festival. Not only *at* the Film Festival, mind you, but actually walking into the foyer of the State Theatre on the red carpet reserved for visiting megastars. She thought a bit, then sat down and typed another message which said, 'I don't care about you taking her to boring functions like the Film Festival but it's a bit off swaggering down the red carpet with visiting nobodies.' She thought about the signing off bit and added, 'Chiz, Iris.' This seemed about the right tone still.

She sent it by courier to his office and his secretary, Susan, rang to say that he had just left for a month's holiday in Vanuatu with Barbara and had Iris met her, and wasn't she a nightmare. (This meant that Susan had opened the envelope marked 'personal' and read the message, but this is what the secretaries of old libertarians do.)

Then Sal phoned Iris. She had been making enquiries on Iris's behalf to find out who exactly this Barbara was. She had asked around Sydney and had made several phone calls to the United States of America. She had phoned her and Iris's mutual friend Brenda in her Village loft.

'Brenda said she's vile,' said Sal. 'Thick as two planks. Bone-headed.'

'How does Brenda know her?'

'Well, she doesn't, well not very well really. Pete apparently lived with Barbara for the year he was on sabbatical in New York and Brenda met her once or twice then. When I first asked what she was like, Brenda said she was OK, but when I told her about you and Pete she changed her mind and said she was awful. She even rang me back the next night to confirm it. She said she had once had dinner with them in their apartment and Barbara cooked the worst meal she'd ever eaten, and only served one bottle of wine with dinner and then offered them Bailey's Irish Cream with the coffee. *Bailey's*! And put the cork back into the red wine at the end of dessert and put it in the fridge, sorry *ice-box*.' Sal did an exaggerated New York accent on this, then added, 'And I suppose she's a secretary in some department at Rutgers.'

Iris said that underneath it all Barbara was probably

97

very nice. And in any case she didn't really care.

'Ring her,' Sal urged. 'Tell her to piss off and stop pestering him. That she's an embarrassment to him in Sydney. That she might have been alright for him in New York when he was lonely and couldn't get anyone else, but that she's an *embarrassing nuisance* in Sydney.'

A month later Iris rang Pete and suggested they have lunch at the New Hellas. They sat at the blue linen covered window table and looked down over Hyde Park and up to Whitlam Square. The trees waited in the heat for the southerly as the lunchtime office crowds moved desultorily along the shimmering asphalt. Pete smiled at her and they both looked out the window again. They had taramosalata, tzatziki, kalamata olives, anchovies, kalamari, thick white crusty bread and two bottles of Demestica, followed by big glasses of Metaxa which the proprietor gave them gratis because they had been eating and drinking there on and off for years. As they ate and gazed out on to the trees, they talked about Iris's business, which was going downhill a bit, and Iris asked him about his book-in-progress on William Gass. They discussed movies they'd seen recently, Ernest's new girlfriend from Canberra who was driving him mad wanting to have babies, the hostages in Lebanon, the Adelaide Arts Festival and Pete's ex-wife who, he said, was at last pulling herself together and going out with other men. Iris was cheerful, drank too much and talked very fast. Her palms were sweating. At 3.30 when Pete said he had to leave to go to a meeting, they stood up and took the old clanking iron lift down to the ground floor in silence. On the hot footpath, he kissed her abruptly on the cheek and said, 'You're a class act, Iris.'

Iris went back to the office with a splitting headache from the tension and nausea from the booze.

Over the next few months Iris heard quite a lot about

Barbara. Dozens of Sydney women kept her up to date on things.

Sal said she'd run into her at parties a few times and had made a point of talking loudly to Pete about how well and young Iris was looking these days, how successful she was, and how she was making pots and pots of money.

Carol said, 'She's quite nice, Iris, quite pretty, I suppose, but she doesn't wear clothes like us. She wears, um, sort of crimplene. In kind of, um, pastel colours.'

Jenny said, 'I saw her sitting on Pete's knee at Ernest's birthday party, it was a truly disgusting sight.'

Di said she went to a dinner party with them and everyone talked about post-modernism in Australian literature so Barbara couldn't join in.' (Iris wondered how *any* of them could discuss Australian post-modernism but was grateful for the information.)

Jenny said, 'She reads Morris West, Anna called round at the house and caught her, I suppose that's her idea of Australian literature.'

Helen commented that she would have thought Colleen McCullough more her cup of tea.

Corrie said she'd had a party and Barbara had brought *a plate*! An awful meatloaf thing she'd gone to the trouble of making herself.

Prue said she looked as if she used a blow dryer on her hair *every day*.

Patricia said she looked as if her life had been an endless battle with her hair.

Sal said she'd heard from Susie who'd heard from Ernest's Canberra girlfriend that she'd painted Pete's bathroom a terrible orange and lowered the value of his house.

Corrie said she probably had to stay at home to paint the house because no-one would talk to her when she went out with Pete, including him.

Mary said you could tell she wanted to marry Pete,

you know what American women are like, and that was
why she was staying in Sydney so long but you could tell
Pete didn't want to marry her.

Sal said imagine what the babies would look like.

Prue said she was the epitome of American mommism.

Carol said Pete looked as if he was going broke having
to pay for her awful taste in everything and that after she
went back Corrie would have to have a fund-raising
party for him in her restaurant.

Iris said, 'Look, he must *like* her. He must have *asked*
her to come to Sydney, she wouldn't just come here on
spec,' but they all said nonsense, she'd just arbitrarily
inflicted herself on him – and worse, on *them*.

Sal found a cartoon in *Playboy* which had a picture of
two fat men talking in a bar. One was saying to the other:
'Pam's a snappy dresser, a great talker, a good com-
panion, fancy dancer and cooks like an angel, but Anne
lets me come in her mouth.' Sal whited out the names
and paid for a professional typesetter to substitute Iris for
Pam and Barbara for Anne, then photocopied the *Playboy*
page to send to Pete.

Corrie told Pete not to bother bringing Barbara into
her restaurant again.

Ernest's Canberra girlfriend told Ernest she wouldn't
go out with him again if he stayed friends with Pete.

Sal found out that Pete had gone to a seminar in Perth
for a few days, so she went to the GPO and paid $80 to
have the cartoon facsimiled through to the fax machine at
the Perth Parmelia where he was staying.

After another month Pete phoned Iris and said, 'Um,
it's me. Feel like dinner?'

So Iris said yes and they went out to Kinselas and then
on to Arthur's night club just like they used to. They

didn't mention Barbara until Pete said at the end of the third bottle of Moet, 'Your place or mine?'

'Yours is closer,' said Iris, 'if it's available.'

'She's gone back to New York.'

'For how long?'

'I don't really know.'

'Didn't she like Sydney?'

'It wasn't that, really. It just didn't *suit* her, but I suppose you know that.'

'Nup, didn't really hear anything about her. Don't you *really* know when or if she's coming back.'

'No.'

'Oh well.'

And so they went back to his place because, as Iris said, it was closer, and as he agreed, it was available.

All In The Family

Rosemary Creswell

It was one of those steamy Sydney nights a few years ago when Iris still lived in her ancient harbourside flat before it burnt to the ground. She was at home alone and even with all the windows open no sea breeze lifted the dull heat. She lay on the floor watching a PGR *Dynasty* episode. It was the non-rating period which always made Iris think that whatever you did in those few months didn't count, had no status.

The phone rang. She wondered whether to bother to answer it, then did.

It was Ernest. On a public phone. She hadn't heard from him for months. 'Iris. Um, Howard and I are having a few drinks and thought if you were on your own and doing nothing we might call over.'

Iris smiled.

'I know what you're up to, Ernest,' she said, 'and no, I'm not interested. But if you're only up to me in your little black books, try the whole alphabet and if you don't have any success, come over anyway and have a drink. It's probably a bit cooler than wherever you are.'

Ernest said he might ring back later.

Iris rang Sal, whose surname was earlier in the alphabet than hers. 'Have they phoned you?' she asked.

'Who?'

'Ernest and Howard.'

'Oh Ernest phoned about twenty minutes ago and said he felt like a drink, but I'm too tired. And I've got the kids this week anyway, so I can't go out. But he didn't mention Howard. Why?'

'Oh they're up to this new trick of theirs I think. I've heard about it from Corrie. For the past few weeks they've been into threesomes – the two of them and a woman. It's amazing what success they seem to have had. I've heard of lots of women who've been in it. People you'd never imagine would do it. Just amazing. But they're only up to me so far, so they've got a long way to go in their phone books.'

'You wouldn't do it, Iris, would you?' asked Sal.

'Don't be daft, of course not. But I've told Ernest if they have no luck they can come over anyway for a drink. Anyway, you can't have orgies with your oldest friends. It's like all that awful middle-class American wife-swapping. God knows how they can do it and keep a straight face.'

'Well hardly,' said Sal. 'It's a bit different, isn't it? I mean, two chaps and a sheila?'

'Oh well, if the kids go to sleep and you feel like coming over, do.'

By the time *Dynasty* was over, Iris was wondering whether to go to bed or go for a walk along the harbour wall to see if there wasn't just the hint of a southerly breeze coming.

The front door bell rang, and through the rippled lead-light of the door she could see two largish male shapes, distorted by the glass.

She let them in. They were each carrying a bottle of bourbon and they looked a bit sheepish.

'No go, eh?' said Iris, getting out some glasses.

'Sweetheart, we don't want anyone except you,' said Howard, giving her a big bear hug. 'We're not interested in just *anyone*. We've got a bit of class you know.'

103

Howard still had his business suit on, crumpled as usual and ill fitting his large bony frame. His collar points were curled up, and his shirt hung down below his loose-fitting jacket at the back, with a button missing at the front. Howard had his own business as a stockbroker. He was very rich and although he was very clever his friends wondered how he made out with the people from that world who wore neat pin-striped suits and university or club ties. But somehow he managed not only to have those people in awe of him but to make a lot of money, which he squandered generously on his friends. Over the years he had bought a lot of valuable Australian paintings, and when someone he liked was broke he would give them a painting and tell them he was sick of looking at it on his wall and would they like to have it or sell it when they got sick of it. He was one of Ernest's closest friends. Indeed, over the years he had been Ernest's patron, looking after him in between royalty payments and film deals. But he was always gracious about his loans to Ernest, calling them an investment in Australia's literary future and congratulating himself on having the foresight to invest in such a valuable long-term property.

Ernest frowned at Howard and said, 'Look Iris, we're not here for that. We've stopped all that. It got boring. We just wanted to see you and have a drink.' And he filled the glasses to the brim with Jack Daniels.

They played country and western music and drank and then Ernest, who for the first time had recently bought opera season tickets and was 'into' opera, wanted to hear *Fidelio*, so they played that and then the whole of *The Magic Flute*, and kept talking and drinking. But there was still a strange edge to the evening. And no southerly had arrived to cool things down.

By three a.m. they were all very drunk, lying on the floor and still talking. Iris wondered if perhaps she hadn't asked them over to see what would happen after all. To see if she could do it. But she didn't think she could, not with friends.

Things fell into a hole of silence. Then Iris said, 'Well I'm tired and think I should go to bed, and you can both stay here but you can't sleep in Peg's room because she's probably coming home some time, so if you want to you can both sleep with me, but *sleep*.' She said this in a rush, not looking at them, as she stood up and walked into the kitchen with her glass.

'Good thinking, sweetheart,' muttered Howard.

In Iris's bedroom they undressed awkwardly, Howard falling over as he tried to take his socks off standing up. Then they got into Iris's queen size bed with Iris in the middle. They turned the light off. Then they lay there, tense. No-one could do anything. No-one could say anything, and no-one could go to sleep. Iris got up and turned the light on, deciding what she needed was a cigarette. She climbed back in between them, and with the ashtray on her stomach, puffed away, trying to look relaxed. Howard leant over the side of the bed and extracted a huge Cuban cigar from his twisted up coat on the floor and lit it. The pungent swirls of smoke rose in the still hot air. They were all perspiring but Iris insisted on keeping at least the sheet up over them. Then Ernest decided he had better have a cigar too. Iris had never seen him smoke in his life.

And so they lay there, not talking, puffing away, with Howard and Ernest ashing their cigars in the ashtray, and Iris could feel the heat of the ash on her stomach through the amber glass ashtray and the sheet. When she finished her cigarette, she closed her eyes, moved the ashtray on to Howard's stomach, and yawned loudly. Then she leant over and switched off the light.

'You two can finish your cigars but I'm going to sleep,' she said, yawning again. Then she lay there on her back – she *never* went to sleep on her back, it gave you bad dreams – and made loud deep breathing noises, much louder, she realised after a minute or two, than when you are really falling asleep. She must have sounded as though she was having a heart attack. So she tried to soften the noise and slow the breathing down. But her heart was beating, she could feel it, even hear it, she thought. Her arms lay stiffly at her sides.

When Ernest finished his cigar, he took her hand in his, shyly almost, and they lay there hand in hand on their backs with their eyes closed. Like children.

Iris was panicking. I'm not drunk enough, she thought, to do this. She wished Howard would get out of bed and go on to the couch in the lounge-room, but she wasn't game to tell him to. She didn't even know if she could speak. She thought if she tried to say anything, only a funny squeak, or nothing at all, would come out.

She decided the best thing to do, if something was going to happen, was to pretend she was so drunk she was unconscious.

While she and Ernest were holding hands, Howard loomed over and kissed her. She held on tight to Ernest and screwed her eyes closed even harder. Howard moved his hand down to her thighs and she parted them. She held her breath for so long she almost *could* have had a heart attack. She tried to look more unconscious, though she found herself squeezing Ernest's hand, for comfort or out of some kind of proxy sexuality she couldn't tell.

Then Howard rolled over on to her and they had a sort of a fuck with Ernest still holding her hand tightly. He squeezed it, in a sort of reassuring way. It wasn't what you could honestly call a fuck, with Iris lying there rigid, holding her breath and the hand that wasn't holding Ernest's clenched. And Howard's heart, she could tell, wasn't in it. She wondered if this was how it usually was, with the other women who had done it, but she supposed not. After a few minutes he rolled off her. She couldn't even tell if he had come, not until the morning when she saw some damp on the sheet.

Ernest kissed her softly on the cheek and rolled over towards the wall and went to sleep. Iris curled into his back, and then Howard rolled over too and curled into her back. Iris, lifting her head, could see the first light on the distant sea-line through the window, and shivered as she felt the brief slice of cool that comes just before sunrise. As Howard softly snored, she too fell into a deep sleep, feeling strangely safe as she drifted off, as though she had two big brothers protecting her.

When she awoke at seven, it was already hot again. The southerly hadn't come. It was going to be another Sydney scorcher. Howard was struggling into his even more crumpled clothes and Ernest was already dressed, drinking coffee and looking out the window at the grey glass harbour.

Iris looked at her watch. 'There's a ferry in five minutes,' she said. She wondered what on earth she looked like. She could feel the bourbon fumes in her mouth still, and could hear a record still going round and round on the turntable in the lounge-room. The sheets were twisted down at the bottom of the bed and she leant down and pulled one over her. 'If you hurry you'll catch it.'

'Come on, Howard,' Ernest urged, 'I've got work to do today.'

'OK, OK,' Howard said grumpily, 'I'm coming. It's alright for you, you don't have to wear a suit to work.'

As they let themselves out of the front door, Howard, still struggling with his shirt buttons, turned to her and grinned as he waved a warning finger at her.

'Now don't forget, honey, our reputations are at stake, we both fucked you eight times, got it?'

'Got it,' she said.

And as she lay back in bed she could hear them running

107

down the hill towards the ferry wharf. She drank a glass of milk and went back to sleep.

That night she had to meet a publisher in the Journalists' Club. She didn't go to work all day, but in the late afternoon she showered and ironed a silk shirt and linen skirt and dragged on her stockings still wet from having washed them in the shower. She washed and conditioned her hair and blew it dry and applied her makeup. She picked up her briefcase, put her notes in it, clipped some earrings on, sprayed Arpège all over herself, and caught a taxi to Chalmers street. The publisher was from Melbourne and was dressed in a wool flannel suit and wearing an old boys' tie.

As they were discussing things over gins and tonic, she looked up and saw Ernest arrive, with the chief-of-staff of a Sydney newspaper. Ernest was dressed in a suit too, and carried the best of the many briefcases which he had for different occasions. They sat at a table some distance from Iris, and as Ernest got up to go to the bar he winked at Iris. She smiled back. The publisher asked who he was and she said, 'Oh, that's Ernest Houseman, the Sydney writer.' The Melbourne publisher said he hadn't imagined from his writing that Houseman would look like that. He thought he would look more informal.

The following day, Sal called into Iris's office for lunch.

'Well, where were *you* all day yesterday?' she asked, smiling, curious and mock curious.

'In bed,' said Iris. 'Asleep. Alone.'

'Did they come over?' Sal insisted.

'Oh yes, they came over.'

'Did you do it?'

'I'm supposed to say I did it eight times. With each of

them. They've got a name to live up to.'

'Yes, but did you do it at all?' Sal wanted to *know*.

'No. Well, yes, sort of, but no.' It was hard to really explain.

During the afternoon Ernest phoned her and said he was in the pub up the road and would like to meet her for a drink. Iris told him she could be there by six if that wasn't too late.

Over beers, he said, 'Iris, I just want you to know that I don't really think of you as like the other night. You know how I've always felt about you. You know that if things were different we could have a great and wonderful affair, and maybe we will some time. Not now, because of all the complications of my life, but maybe another time. You know how much I admire you.'

Iris said, 'We love each other, in a kind of way. I think we always have. But we don't ever have to do anything about it.'

'Yes, but it's just that I don't want the other night to have spoiled things.'

'It hasn't,' Iris said. 'Look I can't stay much longer, sorry, I'm having dinner with John. I'll buy a roadie.'

'That's OK,' said Ernest, 'I've got a business meeting with Howard.'

As Iris returned from the bar with two Victoria Bitters she found Ernest flicking through his little black book, his brow furrowed, intent on the task at hand.

'Jesus,' she said, 'you and Howard are certainly not into forward planning are you?'

'It's called sexual crisis management,' he said.

Friends and Lovers
Jean Bedford

Sal had known Mick for over twenty years. They met in their first year of university, had shared student houses, had seen each other through some bad times and some good times. They had, in a way, grown up together, though as they got older they often didn't see each other for months on end. For the last ten years or so they had been in different cities. Sal had married, Mick had lived for years with a woman called Elena, but Sal always thought of Mick as one of her oldest and closest friends, so when she heard he was coming to live in Sydney she was delighted. She liked all her friends to be in one place, available.

She felt the usual upsurge of affection when she came into the restaurant and saw him – his familiar leanness, the craggy Australian face that reminded her of her father's, the inevitable cigarette in the long nicotine-stained fingers. They laughed to see each other and embraced.

'G'day, mate,' he said.

'Hi. How *are* you? It's great to see you.'

The other people at the table watched them as Sal sat down, still holding his hand. She wondered if they thought she and Mick were having an affair. She thought idly, as she was introduced, that it was strange that they never had. They'd spent many nights talking until dawn in the old days, years in the same households, there'd been plenty of opportunity.

It was an easy night. Mick's friends from the film he was working on were amiable and drunken, they welcomed her into the group to the point that, later on, over the final bottle of wine, they were swapping reminiscences, Mick and Sal telling outrageous stories of their radical student days.

'That was fun,' Sal said as they got into her car. 'It's going to be terrific having you here.'

He put his hand on her knee. 'You went a bit quiet on it there for a while. Anything wrong?'

'No.' She squeezed his fingers. 'Just talking – remembering – it suddenly occurred to me that you're one of the few people I know who remembers my mother, and me with her. It made me a bit sad.'

'The old Ethel? Yeah. I always liked her, she was a battler.'

Sal made a face, starting the car. 'She liked you, too. Often said what a nice boy you were – just as well she didn't know about the drugs and depravity.'

They laughed. They shared lots, as Mick said, of formative memories. Sal remembered a night of walking him around and around their sordid Prahran backyard, everybody taking it in turns to make sure he kept walking, didn't lapse into the threatened coma from whatever combination of uppers and downers he was on, him waking up occasionally long enough to mumble 'No doctors. No hospital.'

'Do you remember . . .?' she said.

'Everything. It's a fuckin' curse.'

'Mmm. Perhaps. Shall I take you back to the hotel?'

'What about your place?'

'Probably safer, with the breathalyser and all.'

Later, having smoked his dope and caught up on people they both knew, Sal yawned hugely and said she had to go to bed.

'Where do you want to crash? There's the kids' beds, there's even two rooms with no beds at all since Leo and Spiro moved out.'

He looked at her.

'Or there's mine, if you want to share. But I'll have to find another pillow, the kids keep ripping mine off.'

'OK,' he hugged her and they kissed – old friends.

In bed they lay smoking and talking, holding hands, and Sal could feel the tension gathering between them. Shit, she thought, this is someone I've known my whole adult life, we don't need this.

'Look,' she said, 'are we going to fuck, or what?'

He laughed and cupped his hand around her shoulder. 'Well, I'm always in favour of it, myself.'

'OK then,' she was nervous, she wanted to giggle. 'You start.'

'OK.' He moved to kiss her and began stroking her breast. They both laughed and he rolled away. She leaned over and lit another cigarette. 'I don't know,' she said, 'it seems a bit . . . *rude*, you touching me there. It's easier with strangers.'

'Just think of it as incest.' She could feel his erection pushing against her thigh. She sighed heavily and stubbed out her cigarette.

'Alright,' she said. 'Here goes.' She shifted to face him and they lay for a while pressing against each other, Sal breathing deeply to try to relax. His fingers on her back, her neck, her shoulders, became urgent, digging in; they kissed, she reached for him. She thought of telling him she'd always liked the idea of really skinny men with large cocks, but she thought she might get the giggles again.

'It's very strange,' she said, burrowing into his bony shoulder, shy again now, nearly asleep, 'knowing all about your naughty bits . . .'

They woke in the morning to find themselves still embracing, and this time they fucked without awkwardness, carefully, learning each other.

'Listen,' he said, some nights later. 'Do you want to talk about all this?'

She was horrified, felt herself freeze into wakefulness. 'All what?' He was going back to Canberra the next day, wouldn't be in Sydney permanently for a few months.

'This. Us. I mean, we've always been . . . particularly close, always loved each other. And now . . .'

'No. Don't say any more.' She leaned out of bed and groped for her cigarettes. 'You should know about words. They *make* it so.'

'Dangerous, huh?'

'Yep.' She thought of all the words that had passed between them over all the years. Now, she thought, afraid, it was impossible to talk about what was between them. 'There's nothing to talk about,' she said. 'This is all there is.'

'This, and much more.'

She stroked his head, his fine hair, 'But let's not do the words.'

He knew her well enough to recognise her real anxiety, so he put his arm around her and they slept.

A few days later she was enraged at her own cowardice and what she saw as some sort of betrayal of their long friendship. Of course there had been things to say, important things, and he had wanted them said. They had owed each other the saying of them. She bought a postcard and tried to write some of this feeling to him but the

113

result was extremely cryptic, quoting Lenin, among other things. Bugger it, she thought as she dropped it into the post-box. Oh, well, we'll see.

A week later she met Alan in the wine bar, with Hope in one of her match-making moods. Hope worked in the same set of offices as Iris and she sometimes saw herself as a sort of alternative matrimonial agency. It irritated her to see her perfectly adequate friends remain single.

'He's really nice,' Hope said when Alan got up to buy more wine. '*And* he's single. His politics are sound, too,' she added in a thoughtful voice.

Sal immediately thought she'd go home after the next drink. He did seem nice, and he had an earring rakishly in his right ear, which she always liked, but she thought she had enough on her plate already. Later she found out that he had also been about to leave – Hope had given him exactly the same line about Sal while she was in the Ladies. But in the end Hope got so drunk that they couldn't let her drive herself into the Hilton where she was determined to see her boyfriend. Sal thought it was shaping up to be one of those nights. She was fairly drunk herself. The major problem was Hope's dog who went everywhere with her and usually sat on a bed of blankets in Hope's office. If they took a taxi, they couldn't take the dog. Therefore, Hope said, they couldn't take a taxi. There was a certain logic in this, so they thought perhaps Sal or Alan could drive Hope's car to the Hilton. Unfortunately when they staggered out into the cool night they couldn't find it.

'Well,' Sal said, leaning on the gate-post of another restaurant. 'What are we going to do? Are you sure you parked it there?'

'Yes,' Hope could be very definite most of the time. 'It's alright, it's probably just stolen.'

But the problem of the dog remained. Finally they

solved it by putting the dog back in Hope's office, on her bed of blankets, and Alan went to the Lebanese milk bar and bought her some vegetarian kibbe and some little sausages.

'No self-respecting Glebe dog will eat vegetarian kibbe,' Sal said, and it turned out that she was right. Meanwhile, they got a cab and delivered Hope to the Hilton where it seemed logical to stay and have a couple of drinks themselves. Sal was very pleased at remembering to tell Hope's boyfriend Frank that the dog was in the office, though by this time Hope was denying it vehemently. It was a pity Sal didn't tell Frank that they hadn't been able to find the car, because when he asked Hope where it was later she couldn't remember and got into so much trouble that she left the bar in a huff, collected the dog, and out of blind instinct, the missing car, and drove herself home on auto-pilot, a very dangerous thing to do.

Somehow in the bar at the Hilton, with pipers in Irish kilts and jostling desperadoes looking for a partner for the night, Sal and Alan had begun to hold hands. Somehow it became clear in the taxi home that they were going back to Sal's new house, that Iris had helped her move into and Mick had helped unpack. Somehow Hope had won.

'Tell me,' Sal said to Melissa, Iris's assistant, a few weeks later. 'How do you cope with having a proper boyfriend?'

Melissa was a lot younger than either Sal or Iris. She was also extraordinarily efficient, mature and organised, though Sal had noted lately with some satisfaction that she could be as silly as anyone else after the fourth bottle at lunch. Melissa had had the same boyfriend for years, Sal had not had a proper one for – well, she didn't think she'd ever had a proper one, that you cooked for at your place and who cooked for you at his. She was not at all sure that she was equipped to handle it.

Melissa listened sympathetically, then said, 'Don't worry, Sal. It'll work out. You'll find yourself watching telly while he reads or vice versa soon enough. It's only at first that it takes so much effort. Relax. Enjoy it.'

Sal thought she noticed a gleam in Melissa's eye. Ha! the implication was, there go the champagne and flowers.

'Anyway,' Iris said, 'it won't last.'

'Why not?' Sal couldn't see any reason why it shouldn't last a long time, very pleasantly.

'Because he's available,' Iris said. 'He's not married to anyone else, he doesn't live interstate or overseas, you can go out with him whenever you like, more or less. And he's kind to you.'

Sal and Iris had sometimes talked about how difficult it was to cope with men being kind to you. They had both lived for so long being the kind ones themselves, they almost resented it. Sal had talked to Ariel about it too, at length, over their regular long lunches at the Malaya. Ariel said it was because it had taken women of their generation so long to discover strength in themselves that they were frightened of kindness from men, in case it weakened them again. Now Sal thought of a night recently, with Alan, when she had gone to bed feeling very tense and anxious about other things – and Alan had told her to roll over and he would massage her back, which he did for about an hour until she was relaxed and melting. Then they had fucked, gently, but urgently. Yes, she thought, it weakens you. *They're* not supposed to be able to nurture, it's one of the things that keeps us going, that we are the nurturers. Iris got irritated with Phillip, too, when he washed up her dishes or mowed her lawn or fixed her garden shed.

Now she said, 'Oh well, perhaps you're right. But it's nice while it lasts.'

Over dinner Alan said to her, 'I find this . . . relationship . . . rather difficult. Do you?'

She'd known something like this was coming but had
been avoiding thinking about it. In lots of ways it was an
easy relationship – they saw each other frequently, but
neither minded if the other had something else to do, so it
didn't interfere with other friendships or work, the way
some relationships do. When they did go out, to movies
or to dinner or just drinking, they had a good time. They
made each other laugh, they were very physically affectionate, but Sal knew that in some way it didn't quite . . .
click.

'I find all sexual relationships difficult, in the end,' she
said. 'You'd think I'd be a lot better at it by now, but I'm
hopeless.'

'Yes,' he said. 'But apart from that. Even after a few
months and spending so much time together – it still feels
to me like ships that pass in the night.'

She knew what he meant. It was something to do with
his natural reserve, which normally she might have been
keen to break down, but she knew she hadn't tried, she'd
been grateful for it, for the sense that there were no de-
mands being made. But it had allowed her to build up her
own reserve, too, so that there were often now con-
strained silences in apparently relaxed evenings. Neither
of them would make the move to break them. They were
often formally polite on first meeting, needing a few
quick drinks to be easy with each other. What had been a
relief to Sal, not having to analyse or be impatient over
outcomes had become an anxiety in itself. She had begun
to wonder what Alan wanted: if he was, like her, conva-
lescing emotionally, if he was satisfied with things the
way they were between them. And now, clearly, he was
not.

'It's partly my fault,' she said. 'I find it hard these days to let people very near me.' She knew it wasn't quite the truth, there was Mick's place somewhere very near to her, a place he had always had as a friend but that now seemed to be expanding to fill all the space available. She didn't want to think about Mick – she was seeing him the next day, she would think about it then.

Alan said, 'Where do you think this is going?'

She looked at him across the table and thought how fond she was of him, how much she liked his rather grave face with the bright, greenish eyes. She didn't know where it was going, had assumed it would go on the same way until it eventually petered out into friendship.

'I don't know. It doesn't matter much, does it? Fun at the time and all that.'

He took her hand and stroked it. He looked unconvinced, but before he could answer they were joined by a rowdy political friend of his and the conversation became general and scurrilous.

Sal was meeting Ariel for lunch. She got to the Malaya early and ordered a beer while she waited. She was nervous – Ariel had been through so many of Sal's changes of heart about various men, while she herself, Ariel, seemed to have found an equilibrium that didn't depend on men, or 'love'. But in close friendship, Sal thought, resided complete trust. Ariel might disapprove, might secretly shake her head over Sal's peccadilloes, but she would never withdraw her love and support.

She saw her through the glass windows before she came through the door: blonde, pretty, achingly thin. They kissed and Sal gave Ariel the bunch of budding roses.

'They're South African, sorry,' she said. 'I only found out after I'd paid for them, and they're so lovely . . .'

Ariel had given up drink and sex together a year ago. But she still smoked cigarettes with every breath she drew. She lit one now and ordered Chinese tea with her usual self-parodying grimace.

'Fuck, I'd love a beer,' she said, gazing at Sal's. 'Sometimes I think of heaven – all these beers and whiskies that I've denied myself here, lined up on counters that stretch into eternity . . .'

'Once a Catholic . . .' Sal said.

'Once an alcoholic . . .' said Ariel.

Sal privately thought that Ariel had not been an alcoholic. She thought A.A. had convinced her that she had been. But still, Sal had always subscribed to the 'whatever gets you through the night' principle, and she thought if A.A. meetings helped Ariel come to terms with what it was she needed to come to terms with, then that was her prerogative.

'Well . . .?'

'Oh shit, I dunno.' Sal was uncharacteristically reluctant these days to talk. There seemed to be a block of concrete where once there had been a flood of words waiting to be released. 'Just more of the same, I guess. So boring, don't you find?'

'Darling. You could never be boring to me.' They parodied their affection for each other, squabbled in front of amused witnesses like lovers.

'Darling.'

So they gossiped and caught up on what each had been doing since they last met and lunch passed pleasantly but uneventfully. Friends give each other enormous spaces, Sal thought. We never push and pry. We are patient with each other; we believe there is world enough and time.

'I've been trying to ring you all week,' Mick had said, 'but the little copper coils didn't seem to connect.'

'I've been out a lot.' She tried to look at him and couldn't. 'I've been avoiding you. Avoiding thinking about you.'

'I know the feeling. You could have stayed in.'

They drank, together, swirling the wine in their separate glasses.

'Yet,' tentative, 'you're all I've really been thinking about.'

'I know,' agreeing, they are on the same wavelength, have always been.

'I tried to tell you, in the postcard . . . that it's fucked, but also, I suppose, that I hope it isn't. But I'm afraid to hope that.'

'I know . . .' Did he really know?

'I feel old and tired, Mick. I don't want to go through the motions again, not just for the sake of it. Not for the excitement or the adrenalin. I don't want the fascinating illusion again. I want reality.'

'You know what that is?' He leered at her, he could always make her laugh.

'Not a clue.'

'Can you see a future for us, Sal?'

'Yes,' she looked at him now, 'I can.'

'Well?'

'Well, love and sex and work and . . . space. It doesn't mean it'll happen, though.'

'No.'

But she had said to Iris later that she was fairly confident it would happen. For the first time since leaving Robert, or him leaving her, depending on which of them you were talking to, she thought of living with someone again, sharing lives.

'I've already lived with Mick,' she said to Iris. 'Lots of times. I *know* him, we don't have to go through that prelude of being on your best behaviour. I actually think it might work.'

'You're an incurable romantic, Sal,' Iris said with affection.

Sal had thought she was being extremely unromantic about the whole thing.

Now Mick had gone away again. He'd taken up a writer-in-residency in Queensland; his coming to Sydney was delayed further. 'He's like that,' Sal had said to Iris. 'You never know where he's going to be, or what mad project he'll go off on. I do like that in a person.'

They had not slept together on his last visit, but had met and talked deeply about what the possibilities were for them.

'I find it difficult to trust people,' Mick had said. 'Even you, Sal. It's difficult to trust being in love – we all fall in love so often, whores that we are. Can we wait it through? This urgent part of it?'

'Is it a test?' she said. 'A . . . what did princesses send their swains on? One of those, anyway.'

He laughed, they were standing hugging, he had to catch a plane and they couldn't let go of each other.

'I'll pass it,' she said confidently. 'I'm sure I will.'

'Are you certain enough for both of us?'

'Possibly. We'll see.'

But, as she said to Iris, she was not going to be put in the position of being certain for both of them. Mick would have to make his own decisions. She knew what she knew.

'Are you still seeing Alan?' Spiro asked her in the cafe.

'No. We decided to be just friends. It wasn't working. It wasn't what he wanted, and I felt cheap about it.' She smiled, 'Iris says I'm back in my natural state – longing for someone who isn't here and for something that might never happen.'

'Do you think it will never happen?'

'Oh no. I'm absolutely convinced that we'll live together happily ever after. And you know how wrong that might be.'

Meanwhile, as she waited, she worked and saw her friends, including Alan, and sat with great pleasure in her small fern-fronded garden in the sun, and went to the beach with the children, and found that she was enjoying, more than ever before, living alone.

Business and Professional Women

Rosemary Creswell

Dianna was principal of a large girls' school in the western suburbs of Sydney. Before that, she had been deputy principal of a large high school in the arid western district of New South Wales, and had joined the town's Business and Professional Women's Association. It took some of the loneliness out of living so far away from Sydney and her friends. When the Education Department relocated her back in Sydney, she was working so far away from where she lived that Cabramatta High School seemed as remote as the isolated country town where she had just been. And so she joined the Cabramatta branch of the Business and Professional Women's Association.

It was customary on the meeting of every first Tuesday of the month for a guest speaker to address the women after dinner, and Dianna asked Iris if she would mind being the speaker for the next month's meeting.

'There's no money for it, and the food's awful, and it's very boring,' she said to Iris, 'but just think of what a good mark it will give you when you go to heaven.'

'Oh alright,' said Iris. 'What will I talk about?'

Dianna explained that the members were mostly schoolteachers, that there would probably be only two bottles of wine for dinner amongst the twenty or so women, that the women were certainly not militant

123

feminists or anything difficult like that, and that Iris had to talk for only half an hour or so, after the minutes of the last meeting had been read and other business attended to.

'Just tell them about publishing in Australia,' she said, 'or what literary agents are supposed to do. Anything, but don't go on about women having a hard time of it in business or anything like that, because they don't believe it.'

Iris explained to Di that she owed a debt to the B.P.W.A.

When she was seventeen and started her first job in an advertising agency, having lied during the interview about her skills, she was terrified. It was a large agency, run by clever men who had lots of meetings and said things like 'Let's run it up the flagpole and see how it flies' and 'There's no such thing as a free lunch', and 'Advertising keeps the world free'. They knew all about average ratings and cumulative ratings, market leaders, consumer impact, consumer recall, loss leaders, proof of purchase, spot advertising, socio-economic categories, single shot approaches, blanket campaigns and scatter gun techniques. It all sounded a bit like a war to Iris.

The only woman there who had an important job was Olga Brown, a stout woman in her fifties who was company secretary and accountant. She had her grey hair neatly cut in a pudding bowl style, had a fine line of grey down across her upper lip and wore tailored jackets with pleated skirts and sometimes a tie with her linen shirts.

After Iris had been floundering about for a week not knowing what she was supposed to be doing in something called the Media Department, Miss Brown had asked her if she would like to stay back after work and have a drink with her. She told Iris what she would be doing. She patiently explained what the job was. She showed her how to look up a set of reference books called A.A.R.D.S, which stood for Australian Advertising

Rates and Data Service and which told you how much it cost to put an ad in any newspaper or magazine in the country or a commercial on any radio station or TV station in any city (there was no country television in those days). She told her what single column inches were, that T.R.H.P. meant top right hand page and you had to pay a loading for it. She explained what stereos and mats were, and that they had to be delivered to newspapers before they went to bed.

And over the weeks, with Miss Brown's encouragement and guidance, Iris got to learn how to do things and began to earn the grudging praise of some of the men there, even to the point where one Friday night a Mr Packer, who was the son of another Mr Packer, came in for drinks in the boardroom and was looking for someone to take to the Harold Park Trots that night, and the account executives suggested that Iris would fit the bill. She was asked to go up to the boardroom to meet Mr Packer and have drinks with him. She had been doing this nervously for half an hour, the only girl in a room of a dozen men, when the internal phone rang and it was Miss Brown telling the Managing Director that Iris had to urgently return downstairs to work back for five hours. The Managing Director said that he had arranged a prior engagement for Iris, but Miss Brown was adamant and insisted on Iris's return to work.

When Iris went back to the first floor, Miss Brown told her to go home. Iris was forever grateful to her.

The point of all this was that Miss Brown was an Executive Officer of the Business and Professional Women's Association, and frequently went to their meetings in town. She protected Iris from any mistakes she might have made, such as going out with young Mr Packer, and generally helped her get on with her career in advertising, so Iris had fond memories, by association, of the B.P.W.A. Di thought the members of the Cabramatta branch of the B.P.W.A. would enjoy hearing how she

125

got her start in advertising through, the help of a B.P.W.A. woman. Some of them might even have known Olga Brown.

So the first Tuesday of the next month came round, and Iris, who was nervous about public speaking, caught a taxi to the Waratah Motel in Cabramatta where the meeting was to be held. She was early and drank a few Scotches at the bar in the dining-room. Presently other women, mostly elderly, arrived and sat in armchairs and talked to each other. Iris supposed these were B.P.W.A. women, but was too reticent to ask. At last Dianna arrived and introduced her to everyone and they moved into the large private dining-room reserved for their meeting.

A woman called Sue, of Iris's age, called the roll and read the minutes of the last meeting. Dinner, consisting of braised sausages and mashed potatoes and thick white bread and butter sandwiches, was served together with a glass each of moselle. After dinner the women voted on a few issues concerning the forthcoming Christmas party. There was argument over whether they should use a caterer or bring plates, and how the ones who didn't have cars, which was most of them, would have to carry their plates on buses and trains to the party, and what if some of them duplicated plates and there would be more scones than cheese biscuits or vice versa. There was a protracted discussion about whether their annual book voucher prize to a nearby underprivileged school should be increased from ten to fifteen dollars. One of the women felt that, at fourteen dollars a head, sausages and mash was not good enough and should they talk to the motel management about it, but the general opinion was that they were lucky to be able to hire the private dining-room and they shouldn't cause trouble.

Sue then read the correspondence, which was a letter

from a member holidaying in New Zealand who had broken her hip and was having to spend the entire time in hospital but things weren't too bad because she had a lovely view of the Auckland hills, but she was missing the meetings.

Then Sue coughed and said she had a delicate matter to raise. She had received a letter from the Head Office of the New South Wales B.P.W.A, who were concerned about the lack of younger women joining the organisation. Members were asked to participate in a recruitment drive to enrol younger women, and women in a wider variety of occupations. There were too many school-teachers and too many older women in the organisation, it said. It went further. It said that as from one month's time, women who were not gainfully employed could no longer be members.

The women looked at each other in bewilderment.

'That means,' said Sue, 'that as from one month, Dianna and I are the only ones in this branch eligible to remain members.'

All the other women were retired school principals or librarians. The definition of gainful employment was having a full-time salary. Eighteen of them didn't.

There was a hurt silence for a while. One of them, Eileen, said that the local aged citizens Sunset Club had Housie once a month and perhaps they could go there. Violet, who had been the headmistress of Sydney Girls High and who had won the university medal for Latin in 1931, said they could come to her house for supper once a month, but most of them said it was too far from transport and it wouldn't be the same. Doris said perhaps they could arrange for occasional theatre parties, but Mary and Jean said that modern theatre had gone to the pot. They were nonplussed. None of them could think of a solution.

Eventually Iris said that although it was none of her business, she felt that the directive from Head Office was

ageist and unfair, and why didn't they contest it, write a
letter of protest, explain that it was discriminatory.

They looked appalled. They couldn't do that. Head
Office was full of younger women who had really important jobs, and you couldn't go against them.

Iris then suggested that they write to Head Office pro-
posing that there should be associate membership for
retired women, at a reduced membership rate, but which
would still entitle them to most of the association's
benefits. Point out to Head Office that they were the
pioneers of the organisation. That they established that
women could have careers in their own right. That they
shouldn't arbitrarily be put out to grass.

This was considered for a bit, but no-one would vol-
unteer to write the letter.

In an atmosphere of doom and resignation, Iris then
addressed the final meeting of the Cabramatta branch of
the Business and Professional Womens Association. She
had managed to signal to Dianna to get a large carafe of
reisling after dinner and had consumed a fair amount of it
during the minutes, correspondence and announcement
of the branch's demise.

She told them the story of Miss Brown. Then she told
them what literary agents did. She told them about publishers in Australia. She explained about the role of edi-
tors. Nothing she said evoked a spark of interest. They
listened attentively to her, but they looked as if she was
singing the executioner's song. They were on death row
and they knew it.

At the end they clapped politely, and Dianna made a
short speech thanking her.

'As it's apparently our last meeting,' said Dianna, 'why
don't we all have a drink, a sherry or something.'

They looked at each other dubiously, and one or two
of them nodded. Dianna and Sue managed to procure
from the management two cut glass decanters of sweet
sherry and twenty-one glasses. Most of the women

sipped gingerly at the yellow liquid served in **pony** glasses.

For a while not much was said. The retired majority politely asked the two employed B.P.W.A. women about their jobs and how they liked the proposed new term system for schools. Some of them re-applied their makeup. They clasped their faded brown hands together, heavy gold rings on some of them, and clutched their damp handkerchiefs in their palms. They snapped their snakeskin handbags open and shut noisily. One or two of them were beginning to stand up to go, when a few others tentatively began to ask Iris questions, about who were the new young women writers in Australia.

One of them said that she had read that when Christina Stead died, the papers said she had been unrecognised in her own country, and did Iris think that was true, because she felt personally she had been given a lot of recognition, certainly as much as she deserved.

'You remember her, Violet,' said Doris, 'at high school. Wasn't she *awful*? Winning prizes and things all the time.'

The women who were about to leave sat down again.

Violet nodded and took a second or two to swallow her mouthful of sherry. 'And writing about poor men of Sydney, as if she'd know much about it. Came from a privileged background, with a rich father. Had better clothes than any of us. And just as bad at university too. In the library all the time, and winning all the essay awards.'

Doris got the giggles, and then the hiccoughs, and Enid had to smack her on the back.

'Someone,' said Mary, 'said that Dymphna Cusack was supposed to be a successful writer, but I don't know anyone in Australia who's read her. When I was in Russia everyone was talking about her. But who'd want to read her *here*? I mean I've *read* her because I thought I'd better if everyone in Russia was reading her, but I can't see why she's cracked up to be all that good. You were at university with her Madge, weren't you? What was she like then?'

'Off always at the Left Club meetings and things. They weren't too bad I suppose, but I didn't get to many of them. They were the days. Lots of parties and picnics, and getting into trouble all the time for getting home late. But I remember Dymphna. Had a lot to say for herself, as I recall.'

'I knew a girl once, turned into a writer. Barnard something. Double-barrelled name.'

'No, that was two people,' said Mary. 'Barnard *and* Eldershaw. *A House is Built.* Except that they joined them together to sound as if they were one person. Funny two people writing the same book. You'd think they'd have fights about it. I couldn't even share writing a school report with someone let alone a book.'

Ada, who had been a school librarian, said, 'Don't think any of them were that good really, we had all their books in the library but hardly anyone ever borrowed them.' She reached across for the decanter.

'Judith Wright's still writing. Still churning out poetry,' said Enid, then slapped her hand on the table. 'Never stops, should call her Judith Wrighting.' She laughed and took the decanter from Ada. 'Anyway, you write much better poetry than her, Doris.'

Doris looked down at her hands modestly and then held out her empty glass to be filled. 'Oh I only do it for myself,' she said. 'Not so full of myself that I'd inflict it on anyone else.'

'I've read some of your poems,' said Violet, dabbing up sherry from her lap with a lace handkerchief. 'It's very good. You should get it published.'

'I can remember another writer,' said Ada. 'Jean Devanny was her name. I don't think anyone's heard much of her since, but when John and I joined the Labor Party she was in it. Very *rude* woman, as I remember.'

Ada violently shook the decanter to drain the last drops from it.

'Oh there were lots of them around then, women writers I mean,' said Dorothy. 'That Miles Franklin started the fashion.'

Iris felt someone softly tapping her shoulder. It was Violet standing behind her. She cupped her hand around her mouth and whispered in Iris's ear. 'Doris's poems are really very good, she'd like you to look at them some time.'

Doris was blushing. 'Sit down Violet. I don't want *anyone* to read my poems.'

'And what about you, Ada?' Violet pointed an accusing finger at her. 'I remember when you used to be writing a novel in a school exercise book in the staff room. What happened to that?'

Dianna left the room to order more sherry.

'I know,' said Violet, 'why don't we have a literary group that meets regularly? You know, instead of the B.P.W.A. We could bring along our things and read them to each other.'

'Yes,' said Mary, 'let's forget about the dratted Business and Professional Women. Let them have their silly young business girls in it.' She fell into silence. She'd never said anything so heretical.

Dianna returned with two more decanters. They all held out their glasses eagerly.

The final meeting of the Cabramatta branch of the Business and Professional Womens Association took on new life. The conversation burgeoned. They all talked at once. The private dining-room of the Waratah Motel was host to a flowering of dormant memories, and host to the newly formed literary group.

Iris slipped out unnoticed. She had promised Sal she'd meet her in the Harold Park Hotel in Glebe where Sal was giving a reading from the stories she and Iris were writing. Sal's reading was over by the time Iris arrived, and Sal was in the back bar drinking schooners with her new boyfriend, Alan, who was kind and handsome and wore an earring in his left ear.

'How'd it go?' said Iris, kissing Sal on the cheek.

'OK, good audience,' said Sal, 'how were your lot?'

'Terrific,' said Iris. 'Just like us, only older.'

The Last Word

Jean Bedford

The day Sal learned she did not have breast cancer was also the day she got a letter from Mick saying they were Heloise and Abelard.

She had gone home in the late afternoon after her doctor's appointment to feed her cats and had found his letter in the box. She read it in the car after she parked near Iris's office – they were going to drink champagne with a favourite client of Iris's while he signed his lucrative overseas contract.

She came into the office white-faced and shaking and wondered at the shock on Melissa's and Iris's faces as they looked up from their separate telephones. Then she realised they thought it was the doctor who had caused her wild eyes. She mimed 'mastitis' to them with a twisted smile and touched her breast. She got herself a large white wine from the office kitchen and sat by Iris's desk while she finished her phone call. She drank the wine very quickly, with trembling hands, the letter crumpled somehow around the glass.

Iris put the phone down. 'Well, what's the matter then?'

Sal was so angry she could hardly speak. 'It's . . . I've had this mad letter from Mick. Heloise and Abelard! Tragic karma! Apart for twenty years and yearning for each other, so that's the way it's got to be forever. Fuck.'

Iris made a face, 'What a romantic.'

'What a bull artist! He's decided not to come to Sydney now, he's going to stay in Queensland. He's found a simple way of living there, where he can work and brood about what could have been but was never meant to be . . .'

'Send him a telegram telling him he's a fuckwit and you're disregarding the letter.'

'He tells me not to write to him. That's what makes me so mad, not having the right to reply. How dare he tell me not to write!'

'Do it anyway.' Iris sometimes had a similar problem with Phillip, who would pull his phone plug out when they had an argument so he always got to have the last word. She had occasionally resorted to throwing stones at his window or sending urgent telegrams.

'Well, what're you going to do, Sal?'

'I'm going to write to him of course. Is anyone using the little room?'

Iris shook her head and Sal went into the office she sometimes used to work in and sat at the typewriter, reading his letter through again, smiling despite herself at the haiku at the end and the pressed Queensland wild-flower stuck on with transparent tape.

Dear Mick, she wrote, Who the fuck do you think you are, telling me whether I can write to you or not? What on earth makes you think you can get away with making all these dubious statements without argument?

Stay in Queensland, if that's what you want. Marry a hippy and have dozens of flower-children if that's what you want. But don't tell me it's preordained or karmic or a tragic romantic necessity. *Don't* ask me to live with a secret love and pain enshrined in some useless part of me forever. Don't fucking say 'forever' for a start. And get your facts right. Karma is not predestination. It is the sum of all our decisions and choices and we are always making them and it is always changing. We are not the rocks over which the river flows, we are the river – some guru said that. The karmic rune is Odin's rune, the blank rune, the one that says *nothing is predestined*; there is nothing that cannot be avoided. Karma shifts and evolves as we shift and evolve. So if you're going to throw karma at me, throw it accurately. What you *are* throwing is some twisted medieval concept of love and its concomitant suffering that was born of a particular economic and social system – for Christ's sake, you've read the same books as me.

And when you talk of the bitter irony of it all, I do *not* feel like Heloise, I never have. You are rewriting history. I have loved you openly and fondly for twenty years, I have not nursed a secret wound, nor would I. I won't now. If there *is* a bitter irony it is that having loved you and trusted you as a friend for so long I am now this vulnerable to you as a lover. If what is between us is not possible, then it is not possible, because one of us has *decided* that, for our own reasons.

Please think of what *is* possible. Don't close doors that might remain open and say the universe has slammed them on us. Meanwhile, drop dead.

Love, Sal.

She read what she had written and smiled. She hadn't realised she knew so many things about karma. Once she would have been certain that he would read it and laugh and write an equally abusive and arrogant letter back. Now, she didn't know.

She went back into Iris's room where the champagne was flowing. She toasted Dennis's success and flopped with a sigh onto the couch.

'Did you write a letter?' Iris asked.

'Yes. But then I tore it up. He can go to hell in his own bucket.'

Dennis looked at her with his eyebrow raised. 'Oh nothing,' she said. 'Just a courtly love tragedy I'm embroiled in. *Plus ça change, plus ça même chose.*'

Shortly after this Robert came in with Maria and Rosie for Sal to take them to a primary schools choral concert at the Opera House. Robert brought with him an inscribed copy of his latest book for Sal, with an enigmatic message about the date. When she was calm enough to work it out later she realised it commemorated a particularly unhappy period in their marriage. That'd be right, she thought sourly.

On the Opera House steps they met a friend of Sal's who was the mother of one of Rosie's little mates. They groaned at each other in sympathy.

'Stephen wouldn't come,' said Alice.

'Nor would Robert or Sarah. Can't blame them.'

'Mum! Shoosh,' said Maria, laughing. 'You'll hurt the little ones' feelings.'

A year out of primary school, twelve now, Maria was sophisticated enough to at least pretend she was looking forward to the concert. She had dressed carefully for the evening, in the hope of meeting her old teachers, in an op-shop thirties tangerine lace dress with a black V-necked sweater of Robert's, black socks and polka-dotted sandshoes.

Sal saw Rosie shepherded off with the other singers and she and Maria found their seats. She thought she might die of boredom in the next two hours, unable to re-read Mick's letter burning a hole in her bag, forced to seem interested in the program, longing for at least ten stiff drinks in a row. But in fact the sweetness of the hundreds of young voices, the earnest look on Rosie's face as she bellowed the choruses, the unexpected poignancy of Schubert's *Sanctus* interrupting the spirituals and caròls, calmed her.

'Rosie looks happy,' Maria whispered to her. 'She's finally able to sing as loudly as she can with no-one telling her to shut up.'

There was also the distinction of being the only mother there whose daughter was ticked off for talking between songs and made to move to the end of the row in front of a thousand people.

Walking with her daughters along the Quay, a liner at its berth, their arms around each other, laughing at Rosie's 'naughtiness', she knew she would continue to feel calm. 'What a pretty city,' she said, hugging the girls to her. 'Look at all the lights on the water.'

Rosie gave an enormous yawn. 'Everything hurts,' she said. 'My throat hurts from singing, my feet hurt from standing up, my hands hurt from clapping the orchestra . . . Mummy, why do you have to clap the conductor separately?'

'Well,' said Sal, 'I suppose because he's special, he controls the way the orchestra plays.'

'Or she,' said Maria.

'What?'

'Or *she*. It's sexist to automatically call the conductor 'he'.'

'Grandmothers and sucking eggs,' Sal said. 'Quick, let's get that taxi.'

When she had dropped the kids at Robert's she went to the pub to hear the last reader. Iris and Spiro were there, and Otto.

'Just in time,' said Otto. 'It's my shout.'

She pretended amazement. 'Fuck. Otto buys a drink. How've the readings been?'

They were in the back bar, the other one was too crowded and hot. None of the others at the table had bothered to listen to the readings and Sal knew she would be overcome with inertia too, once she had a drink. Never mind, she thought, writers don't really expect other writers to listen to them.

'Sal,' Spiro said. 'Do you know when Mick's coming back to Sydney? He hasn't confirmed his reading date.'

'Never, at last sighting,' she said. 'Write to him.'

'Aren't you in contact with him?'

'Me Heloise,' she said, taking her gin and tonic gratefully from Otto.

'What?'

'You know – Heloise and Abelard.'

'Nup. Me ignorant Greek kid, who were they?'

'Medieval priest and nun. Deathless love. No consummation possible. You know the tune.'

'It sounds very Greek.'

'It sucks, as the kids would say.' She got out her book and gave Spiro Mick's Queensland address. Then she and Otto resumed their argument about an aesthetic model for the twentieth century and after a few drinks she felt a whole lot better. But after a few more she suddenly was very tired and said she wouldn't go on with the others to Iris's place for a nightcap.

'Do you want to crash at my place?' she asked Otto. She thought it would be comforting to have another body in her bed and she knew they wouldn't fuck. But Otto was in a drinking mood so she walked home up the hill in the warm night by herself. She let herself in to the clean empty house and the new kittens came rushing to meet her. Brushing her teeth, the little purring cats climbing round her ankles, she looked into the mirror and thought of all the things she would say to Mick when he came to his senses. At least, she thought, settling between the fresh sheets and turning out the light, at least I'm not about to die of breast cancer. Perhaps me Pollyanna. She fell asleep smiling.

A Thousand Miles From Care

Rosemary Creswell

'It's alright, it's alright Iris. I promise you it's alright. I mean it, truly. Please don't. *Don't*.'

He rocked her. He rocked and rocked and rocked her. They lay in bed, it was Saturday morning, early. She put her head on his chest and she wept and wept and wept. She rocked her head against his shoulder and she rocked her head against his chest. She banged her head on him. She banged her head on him and kept saying I'm sorry, I'm really sorry. I don't know why I'm crying.

She cried in a huge avalanche of sadness. For her and for him, but mostly for her.

She said, 'This is all self pity, it's got nothing to do with you. You shouldn't have to put up with it, I'm sorry.'

She forgot about him for a moment, except that she still knew that if he hadn't been there she wouldn't have cried. She would have pulled up the sheets over her head and said to herself, all you need is a rest. You work hard, you play hard (that's what John used to say to her by way of explaining the frightful emotional messes she would get into) and sometimes we get tired and we need to protect ourselves from the outside world.

And still she kept banging her head on his chest.

She cried about everything that came into her head.

She cried because she had to leave her house because the landlord had sold it. She cried because she knew Phillip wouldn't want to use the chance to say let's live together. She cried because she'd have to do all the moving herself. She cried because Billy her dog had a rash on his chest and it wouldn't go away. She cried because she should have been working harder. She sobbed because she knew she had wasted her life. She thought about all the trouble of packing things up and moving them into a squalid little flat on her own. She remembered that last time she hadn't had to move anything at all because her Kirribilli flat had burnt down and there was nothing to move. She remembered how her friends had helped her and Corrie had had a benefit party for her, and she cried out of gratitude. She cried when she remembered she hadn't cried about all those things when she should have. She cried because she had no right to cry, and that made her cry more. She cried about all the things she should have cried about at the time, but didn't. She wept when she thought how stoic her friends were, and how they never wept.

And still he rocked her against his chest. Cradled and rocked her.

There's a limit to how much you can cry. It reminds you of when you were younger, when you cried and cried and your father said to your mother, 'That girl must have a well behind her eyes, so many tears come out, for no reason.' Though he meant it kindly, she remembered.

So after a while you sob yourself out. The sobs turn into hiccoughs and the hiccoughs turn into coughs and then you disguise them by starting to laugh.

He was so distressed. He kept saying, it's alright. Keep crying if you want to. Cry as long as you need to. But by that time she could imagine what she looked like.

She looked even worse than she thought she would. She got out of bed, laughing, and looked in the streaky mirror. Her face was swollen as if a whole hive of bees had stung her. Her skin puffed. She was bloated up from menstrual fluid retention though you would have thought all that welter of tears would have sluiced off any excess liquid. Her eyes were slits, folded in by squashed up flesh. Her face was pink and blotchy. The tear stains didn't look tragic. She just looked as though she was a fat schoolgirl who'd been crying all day either from having her lollies confiscated or being bullied by the boys at playtime.

After a shower, Phillip made breakfast for her: fresh orange juice, toast and tea. That was what he always had, but muesli as well. He'd been having that breakfast for twelve years.

Over the Saturday papers and because she knew he would be going home to work on his book all day, she said, 'I think I'll get the hydrofoil to Manly and lie on the sand and thrash around in the surf. That's what I'll do.'

She said it almost defiantly.

'Can I come too?' he asked quietly.

'Well of course you can,' she said sharply, almost disappointed that this act of solitary therapy was going to be shared. As if there were some tragic stature in getting the hydrofoil alone to Manly.

On the jerky bus to Circular Quay she was snappy, and he put his arm around her and said, 'Don't be cranky, please.'

'I'm *not* cranky, I'm just sad.'

'Well I have an idea,' he said, 'I'll tell you later.'

At Circular Quay, whether it was because of his promised idea or whether it was because Circular Quay, with its smell of Italian kids illegally baiting their lines from the wharves; its blousy vulgar sprawling mess of pie-selling kiosks and bad pavement artists and buskers; the stale odour of chips and its wheeling cholesterol-bloated seagulls; its wind and ferry-churned water; and its great wonderful Opera House shells already tawdry from the unplanned-for wear and tear of salt water and ozone – she could not tell, but she felt suddenly cheerful. It was as if the wind and the noise descended on what might have been left of her tears and whisked them out to sea forever.

They bought hot dogs with sauce *and* mustard. She told Phillip that was the best way for hot dogs. She was amazed. She'd never seen Phillip eat anything so unhealthy let alone buy it from a junk food stall.

They sat downstairs on the hydrofoil. Iris insisted. It felt more dangerous. The great hydraulic waves of water sprayed and pounded an inch from your face if you pressed it against the glass, which Iris did, having insisted on the window seat. The vessel was only half-full. In front of them sat two men, one middle-aged, one young, talking and pointing out at the opera house.

'Septic tanks,' she said to Phillip, nodding in their direction.

'What?' he said.

'Septic tanks,' she yelled over the engine and water spray noise. 'Yanks.'

Phillip was embarrassed, and he didn't even *like* Americans. He'd never heard the expression before. Iris liked Americans and she'd certainly never used the expression before. She felt as though she was about ten years old. She pressed her face against the glass again.

Phillip was saying something but she couldn't hear him.

'What?' she yelled.

'I said, I've been thinking this morning that I could give up my flat and we could look for a house together. I mean to live together in. We could both look, together I mean.'

She stared at him, shocked.

They were in a sealed unit with walls of water cascad-

142

ing around them. She felt very frightened. She thought of all the muesli breakfasts. Then she thought of all the ordinary, normal, kind, friendly comfort. She worried at the thought of him getting up at exactly 6.30 every morning and listening every morning to the ABC seven o'clock news headlines followed by the 7.15 ABC news followed by the 7.30 BBC World Roundup, then switching to the second ABC station and listening to A.M. then switching to 2MBS music. Then she thought of coming home every night to a warm firm embrace. And she thought of the comfort in bed and wondered if the sex would wear out. She thought of how he was the first man for decades whose face she didn't have to change in her sexual fantasies and she wondered if after a while she would have to make him some other anonymous person like she usually had to do.

She stared out the window again, squashed her nose up against it and reminded herself of how once when she was fifteen she got herself catatonically drunk and the family doctor had said she was like a child with her nose pressed up against the lollyshop of life.

'Well?' he yelled.

She turned around to him slowly. She saw his warm worried face. Then she threw her arms around his neck and said, yes, yes, yes.

They wandered along the Manly Corso. She pointed out some canvas men's shoes in a sale. He went in and tried them on and bought them, and then he bought her some sandals. They told the saleswoman to wrap up the old shoes and they kept the sandals and canvas shoes on until they got to the sick pines and the sand of South Steyne where they undressed and lay in the sun shining intermittently through the clouds.

Iris sifted the sand and let it run through her white winter fingers. Phillip would not go into the water, but she had to: it was a childhood edict from growing up at a beach. You could not lie on the sand and not 'go in'; it was a kind of a crime. The water was icy but she forced herself to stay in and wave at Phillip who was not looking but trying to read the Saturday papers. Another crime. If you grew up on a beach you knew you could not read newspapers or even books on it. Still, he probably had some childhood country stuff he knew about.

After she dried off, she went to the Corso and bought two cans of Victoria Bitter, a half a kilo of king prawns, lemon and bread and butter, and they ate them on the sand. Iris really knew you couldn't do this on a beach either. It was tactically impossible. But the sand on the prawns and the shells blowing away across the beach didn't seem to matter, nor the butter melting in the sporadic sun and dripping with the lemon juice up their arms and getting on Phillip's new canvas shoes lying there looking so innocent, so untested.

They finished their feast and Iris said, unnecessarily, that it was like a wedding breakfast. She went into the cold waves again. Another saying was that you shouldn't go into the water for at least an hour after you have eaten, or you will get stomach cramps, but Iris knew it wasn't true. Only people who didn't grow up in beach suburbs believed that.

When she came out the sun had completely disappeared behind the clouds and Phillip was shivering. They decided to go while there was still some time to look for houses to live in. Having made the decision they might as well start there and then.

They wore their new shoes for house hunting and on the return hydrofoil trip they sat upstairs and outside, even though the sky was lowering, and just before they arrived at the Quay large drops began to splat down on the deck.

'We've been a thousand miles,' said Iris.

'What?' said Phillip.

'It's what the Manly tourist ads used to say: Seven Miles from Sydney and a Thousand Miles from Care.' They smiled and the rain fell and fell.

Not To Be Continued

Jean Bedford

Sal was with the girls at the café on a Sunday morning having their fortnightly brunch. She was slightly hung-over and the sight of Maria's iced chocolate was making her feel nauseous, in a fascinated kind of way. Spiro came in, as he often did, and sat with them.

'Listen mate,' he said, 'are you going on Wednesday night, or not?'

'I don't know,' she said. 'I'm having dinner with Ariel. Anyway, what's it to you?'

He laughed, 'Oh, it's an old Greek custom – if you can't be a protagonist, be a spectator.'

Sal was already slightly worried over how much her friends knew about what was happening with Mick. She sometimes thought that she was the sort of person who didn't deserve a private life. She also knew that Mick would be horrified at the thought of his emotions being any sort of communal property, in the way that Phillip had been when he found out that Iris had told people about his marriage proposal. Still, she basically agreed with Ernest, whom she had heard once giving a talk about the obscenity of notions of privacy, how they were essentially bourgeois and led to fascism, alienation, censorship and Orwell's authoritarian society. She tucked that thought away, for use, if and when Mick ever accused her.

146

'I am not conducting my life for your entertainment,' she said, however.

'Oh bugger,' said Spiro. 'Who *is*, do you know?'

She held out her right palm to him. 'OK, read my hand and tell me what to do.'

'Only if you promise to come on Wednesday,' but he bent over her hand. 'Suppressed emotion!' he said, triumphantly. 'If you don't come, you'll be really pissed off at yourself.'

'What else is new?' Sal ordered her third cappuccino and smoked while the girls shared a huge slice of chocolate mud-cake. 'Oh, of course I'm coming,' she said to Spiro. 'You know what Ned Kelly said at Glenrowan – "I had to see it through . . ."' She stood up, thinking that what Ned had really said was 'I had to see it end.'

She paid the bill and walked back along the steamy hot streets with her daughters, playing their number-plate game.

'Look,' Maria said, 'SSO – "Sal Sucks, OK?" Mum, why weren't you going to Mick's launch?'

'I was. I was only teasing Spiro.'

'Can we come?' Rosie asked – she was cross that she wasn't as quick as her sisters with the number plates.

'No,' Sal said, squeezing Rosie's plump arm. 'You'll be with your dad on Wednesday.' Which leaves me, she computed privately, three days to worry about it with no distractions. Mick's publishers had sent her the invitation, but Mick must have asked them to. Officially she wasn't to know otherwise that he'd even be in Sydney, although she'd guessed from his last letter that it would be this week. She decided not to think about it at all until Wednesday night – perhaps she really wouldn't go. They let themselves into the stuffy house and as she opened the windows she laughed at herself.

'What's funny?' Sarah asked, picking disapprovingly at a coffee stain on Sal's shirt.

'Oh, there's an old Indian, or maybe Arabic, mind-fucking curse that I just remembered. It goes something like – You can think of the monkey, but you must absolutely not think of its tail . . .'

Sarah smiled, 'I think it's a donkey, actually.'

'Probably,' Sal said. It pleased her deeply when the girls displayed their own wide reading.

'What are you trying not to think about?'

'Life. Come on, get your gear packed for Robert's, and tidy your room.'

She walked into the crowded bar and saw Mick immediately. He was talking to Spiro, who kissed her, so that Mick's embrace was not awkward. But she spent the evening in other groups, letting Mick find her if he wanted to and telling herself that she'd leave early, anyway.

'Well?' Mick came to sit in the empty seat beside her.

'Fairly. Yourself?'

He laughed, 'I meant, well, what do you think? I assume you've been getting my letters? You haven't replied.'

'You told me not to. I think you're fucked in the head, if you really want to know.' They smiled into each other's faces. She could see that his urge to touch her was as great as hers to reach for him.

'In what way, exactly? Can you be precise?'

'Oh, just about life and love and karma and choice and wisdom . . .'

'Whew! Is that all? I thought you were serious for a moment.'

'Deadly.' But she couldn't stop smiling at him.

'Shall we talk, then? Later? Over a joint and a drink somewhere?'

'I'm going soon.'

'Good. Let's walk then.'

'Don't you have to stick around? It's your night, after all.'

'No. Come on. There *is* a party later, but you'll come to that, won't you?'

'Probably.' Looking at him she knew she would not, in fact, be able to tell him all the things she had saved up to tell him. She was too pleased that he was here, beside her, and at the knowledge that they would be sleeping together when the night was over.

They drove to the old ferry wharf and got out and sat with their legs dangling towards the water and he made a joint from her dope and they passed it between them and talked of work and friends and theories of existence.

'It's good, isn't it? Being together?' he mumbled into her neck.

'What?'

'It's good. Being together.'

'Just a bit.' She held herself away from him and laughed at him. 'Yes. Just a bit.'

At the party, which was his party, he leant on the fridge and talked to her for hours. They left just before dawn, with the smell of gardenias coming strongly from some hidden courtyard in the semi-industrial street. They went to her house where he made tea and brought it to her in bed. She thought of other years, other early mornings, when they had not been in love but he had made her tea, and she was suddenly saddened at the idea of a future in which it might not happen very often, if at all. They made love intently, seriously, stopping every now and then to stare at each other until they were both lost in their private and shared passion, then they lay and talked, while the kittens ran all over them and licked at their salty perspiration.

'Tell me a story,' he said sleepily. 'Tell me a story with a happy ending . . .'

'Well,' she said, raising herself on the pillow so that she could look at him while she talked, 'well, once upon a time, there was a woman, no longer very young . . .'

'Rubbish.'

'Don't interrupt. She was no longer young, and she had lived alone for a few years, with her children, and she had had a few disasters, as most women her age have had, and so she had decided not to put herself in the way of disaster any more. Are you sneaking off to sleep?'

'Certainly not.' He sat up, too, and they held hands while she went on with the story.

'So she built a sort of fortress, of her friends and her children and gossip and work and all that, and then, lo and behold, this sneaky rat that she had known all her life, demolished it all from within. She hadn't expected that and so she had no defence. She was defenceless. And being defenceless, she let hope creep in again, too, and once hope had been let in all sorts of other creepy crawlies got through the same crack, like wishing, and need, and plans . . .'

'Are you sure this is going to have a happy ending?' He threaded his fingers through her hair in the gesture she had come to realise most expressed his love for her.

'Yep. *I* am, aren't you?'

'It's your story, go on.'

'But he was a contrary devil, which was one of the things she loved in him, and he couldn't just accept love or happiness because that would be too easy. And, though it made her extremely cross, she understood that, too, because she had known him a very long time, and she had even been with him through some of the things that had made him like this.' Sal looked at him carefully, his eyes were closed but now he opened them and frowned at her.

'You know what I mean, don't you?' she said. 'The trouble is, I loved Elena too, still do. And you were very good together in lots of ways, marvellous together, but you tore each other to shreds in the end, and that's what you are afraid of, aren't you?' He nodded, but his face was no longer open to her.

She went on with her story. 'And this man, who was so fine, so good and kind and beautiful, with an awkward grace that, now that she is in love with him, catches at her throat when she notices it, let himself be . . . I don't know, *diminished*, somehow.' She looked at him again. 'You did, you know. You let it happen – you have that quiescent but resentful side to you. It wasn't purely Elena's doing.'

'Don't I know it.' He put his hand over his eyes.

'And,' Sal continued, 'and so he thought it had put him out of the way of that sort of love again, that he couldn't trust himself or anyone else to operate on that deep a level without it meaning destruction for somebody. So he thought he'd just plough on, in a sort of heroic way, alone, with what he was doing . . .'

'Well? Why have you stopped? Is that the end of the story?' His face had a resigned look now, and she thought that she had hurt him. She was surprised to find in herself a fierce feeling, like the one she had for her daughters, that she might want to spend her life shielding him from any more hurt.

'Oh,' she said, and slid down in the bed, kissing the sweaty crease at his thigh, 'I don't know. It's an unfinished story and I'm too tired to make up an ending. Let's sleep now.'

'OK.' He settled himself, too, with his arm around her, but she could feel his tension. She stayed awake until she saw that he slept, and when she tried to turn over his grip tightened on her arm to prevent it.

A week later they sat on the beach watching the dark waves fold in and out under the full moon. In front of them was a cloud filled with lightning, and Sal said idly,

'Isn't it nice of God to arrange a light show for us?'

'Yes. Any moment now Someone might make an Announcement.'

They laughed and stood up together, shaking the sand from their clothes, and walked back to Sal's beach house where prawns and chicken and oysters waited for them. Eating, in front of the big windows open to the sound of the surf and the moon's gilded path across the water, Sal thought savagely of the next day when he would be going back to Queensland. She thought of the weeks of waiting and bleakness before she saw him again, about the promises that had not been exchanged this time, that had been carefully avoided, and suddenly she made her decision.

'I've got cold feet,' she said to him in the car the next afternoon, driving back to put him on his plane.

Surprised, he looked at the floor, and she laughed. 'No. I mean about – us. I don't think I can do it, after all. I think it will have to stop. Until . . .'

'Until?' She could feel his shock.

'Well, until nothing, I suppose. I think it has to be put back in the lap of the gods – I can't carry it any longer.'

He said nothing and she could not trust herself to speak again without crying, so they drove in silence the rest of the way to the airport.

'I won't come in,' she said at the terminal. 'Goodbyes at departure gates are so tacky, don't you find?'

'Anywhere.' He held her face for a moment in his thin hand, lightly fingering the lines beside her eyes, then kissed her. 'I'll send you a postcard or two.'

'Yes, do that. Go well, get some sleep, don't work too hard. Look after yourself.' She could see his grin through her tears.

'It might only be the first chapter, Sal . . .'

'Sure. And we might be reading different books . . .

See ya.' She drove off quickly, not watching him walk into the building, but imagining him, tall, thin, charming, handing his bags deferentially to the person at the counter, then settling with his tobacco and papers at the bar until his flight was called.

And now it's time to stop imagining, she told herself sternly, turning into the traffic on City Road. Now I am going home to get on with things.